Portal to Daske

Secrets of the EYE

Jennifer Liang and Kelly Chang

Chapter 1

Twenty one pairs of eyes watched in anticipation as the minute hand slowly made its way to twelve. It was, after all, the last day of school, and that deserves attention. Even the teacher was bothered, occasionally sneaking glances at the clock while he lectured half-heartedly about the importance of the Quaker Meeting.

Ryan Wexler actually didn't want school to end, because while summer was a long-awaited experience to others, it was considered as a bore to him. At least he had friends in school. During the summer, Ryan was mostly stuck at home with only the TV to keep him company, while his parents worked full time at their home company, Wexler Enterprises.

Granted, he had at least one thing to get excited about. His parents had finally decided, after all those years he had protested, that at the age of fourteen, he was now old enough to take care of himself. Without the Spanish romance loving housekeeper hogging the TV, this summer would be much better. Well, at least better for six days a week, since she still came on Fridays to clean the house. But it doesn't matter, because the housekeeper had no particular love for him and vice versa.

When he finally returned to the world from his thoughts, the bell had already rung and he was one of the few students that stayed back in the now spacious room.

A chubby boy bounced his way to Ryan's desk. "'Sup dude. Whatcha hanging around here for?" he asked.

"Just figuring out what ice cream flavor I should get to celebrate my first day of staying home alone."

The boy shook his head, and then readjusted the pair of oversized glasses dangling loosely on his face. "So, it's the end of eighth grade. Will you consider my advice now? 'Cause you know ninth grade will be like entering a *totally* different world!"

"That's what you told me last summer," Ryan said sarcastically. "And what exactly is the advice you're referring to?"

"About getting a girlfriend, you idiot! You should really think about it! Seriously, if you don't get one this summer, your social status will sink like the Titanic. And you know how mean kids can be in *ninth grade*," he said dramatically.

"Shut up, Roger. You're giving me a headache."

"Aww, come on, man. I just wanna —"

Wincing, Ryan stood up and slung his backpack on his shoulder. "I really should get going. You should, too." He surveyed the empty room and walked out, completely ignoring his friend.

He sighed, and decided to head straight to the smoothie shop. He tried not to think about what Roger just said. Actually, it wasn't that he wasn't interested in girls; there just weren't any that were his type. The girls in his school were mostly the typical blond-hair blue eyes style. Yeah, they were pretty, but he just wasn't interested in them.

Ryan scowled. All of this girl talk was giving him a headache. He debated briefly about choosing a mint-chocolate chip ice cream cone or a fruit smoothie before finally deciding on the latter. After stopping by Mr. Smoothies, he got his triple berry smoothie and headed straight to home.

His house was a gigantic mansion with ten rooms, tall ceilings, and floor-to-ceiling windows everywhere. Ryan's bedroom was actually the whole top floor of the house, and it had everything he wanted. A big screen TV was attached to the wall across his king-sized bed, with sound systems next to it. An elaborate wooden desk stood in the corner of his room, with bookshelves reaching the ceiling beside it. However, his favorite part of the room was what he called "Ryan's Corner", filled with odds and ends like rubber bands, old golf balls, and stuff he used to amuse himself.

He dropped his backpack on the floor and fell onto the bed face down. He was just about to doze off when Mrs. Abdullah barged in with a vacuum cleaner.

She whistled with false cheerfulness and lingered purposefully longer near Ryan's bed. "Such a lovely afternoon, isn't it?" she said with a smirk.

Ryan swore she was just getting her revenge for the TV shows she would miss. Sighing, he muttered, "Can you please turn the volume down?"

"No can do, mister. After all, today is Friday, and it's the only day I can clean this monstrous size of a house from now."

"Since when did you start using a vacuum cleaner?"

"Actually, you're right. Why should I even bother with cleaning when you're the only one living in this house? Oh my, 'Hearts and Chains' is on! You forgot to save your video game again, didn't you? Well, remember to do it again next time!" She abandoned the vacuum cleaner and made a run to the grand living room. She was actually surprisingly fast for a short and stout fifty-five-year-old woman.

2

Ryan sighed again. He had, in fact, forgotten to save his game again, but right now he felt too lazy to move. That woman was probably cackling and yanking out the wires by now.

"Wow. Awesome way to start summer vacation," Ryan said out loud, and heard it echo all over his huge room. Feeling very sorry for himself, he rolled over on his bed and soon fell asleep.

A few hours later, Ryan awoke. When he opened his eyes, he saw a black box perched on his headboard. Surprised, he reached for it, but found that it was sealed tight, with a complicated keyhole in the middle. The box was shaped like a cube with intricate carvings on each side.

Ryan touched one of the carvings, vaguely shaped like a key, when suddenly a purple portal formed on his bedroom floor. It was large enough for a car to fit through, and the way the light shimmered made him see patterns exactly like those carved on the box.

"I must be hallucinating, or I could be dreaming too. Yeah, that's definitely the case. Well, I can do whatever I want in my dream, right?" he thought. Mustering his courage, he stepped forward and fell into the portal.

Clutching the box with both hands, Ryan felt like he was sliding down a gigantic slide that had no end. After a respectable amount of twists and turns, he thought that his stomach couldn't hold it anymore. Much to his relief, the ride gradually became slower and finally opened to a beautiful green field.

A girl with long wavy black hair was staring at him in disbelief. She was wearing a loose fitting pair of white silk pajamas. A delicate ruby pendant held by a thin silver chain hung to her chest. Lying beside her bare feet was a long silvery-white sword embedded with jewels. Moonlight bounced off the blade, reflecting beams of light as if it was a mirror.

The girl took in Ryan's appearance, tall and blond, with a white T-shirt and khaki shorts. A light blush appeared on her cheeks for the slightest second, but vanished immediately when she saw the small black box in Ryan's hands.

Faster than a heartbeat, Ryan found the girl right in front of him, her sword aiming at his throat inches away.

"What are you here for?" she demanded, her ice blue orbs boring into his own hazel pair.

Ryan threw his hands up in surrender. "That's what I should be asking. I don't even know where I am. So can you please remove this sharp thingy? It's kind of unsettling."

She narrowed her eyes and produced a scarlet wand from her pocket. "Bind," she murmured. Chains materialized, tied his wrists, and then made their way to the girl's hand. Giving a tug at the chain and causing him to stumble forward in reaction, she gave a small satisfied smile, ignoring Ryan's wide opened mouth. "I'm taking you to the palace." she declared.

She led him through the winding caverns until he could no longer see the green grassland. The girl, seeing he was busy checking out their surroundings, purposely quickened her pace.

"Can you at least tell me where I am?" Ryan pleaded.

"We are currently at the unmarked lands," she said, "The Council will decide what to do with you when we arrive at Daske. Now shut up, for we're almost there."

Minutes later, she came to a halt. "This is where the Daske border starts. Now, since you are apparently a foreigner, it is technically illegal for you to enter without permission. What city are you from anyway?"

"Er, Los Angeles?"

"Really? Never heard of it. Are you some kind of prince locked in a castle? Daske is the third largest city after all. Surely you're heard of it, right?"

Just as Ryan was about to open his mouth to say no, she continued, "It doesn't matter. But remember, act normal. If you utter one word, I'll leave you with your own mercy. Understood?"

With a wave of her wand, the chains vanished and Ryan suddenly found his fingers intertwined with the girl's. They were just a few steps into the border when they heard a rhythmic march.

"Please show your passes," a soldier said politely. "Or is it the first time for you in Daske?" he inquired, staring at Ryan's "Weirdos Rule!" T-shirt.

The girl reached into her pocket again and brought out a platinum card for him to see. The soldier bowed deeply to her and asked, "And your companion, your highness?"

"I didn't know I needed permission to bring my fiancé to the city. I trust you understand the situation now?" she said icily.

He nodded mutely and soon the whole troop of soldiers lined beside them.

"And what exactly do you think you're doing?" she questioned.

"Escorting you, your highness," he quickly answered. "It's our most honorable duty to ensure your safety."

"If you think you can protect me, don't you think I'm very much capable of doing the same?" she replied, pointedly giving him a look.

"Of course. We'll leave immediately," he said. The soldiers left without another word.

Ryan opened his mouth to ask what was going on, but she cut him off with a cold glare.

"You'll understand later. Shut up."

Ryan wasn't sure what the city looked like because the girl was dragging him around like a whirlwind. In addition, it was midnight, so the streets were all pretty much dark and empty. The girl led him to a black stone wall, "Climb up," she urged, indicating the thick rope hanging down from a window located about five stories high.

"No way," he said, shaking his head. "You're crazy."

The girl huffed. "Come on. We don't have all night. The soldiers must have reported my whereabouts by now. I'll go first then," Nimbly climbing up the wall with the help of the rope, she landed gracefully on the window sill.

Well, if the girl can do it, I can too, he thought. Clenching his teeth, he slowly made his way up.

"Finally," she said, looking annoyed. "Now stay—"

Bang! Bang! Bang! A rapid knocking echoed through her large bedroom.

"Princess! Are you in there?" came a frantic voice. "Open up, Princess!"

The girl cursed under her breath then shoved Ryan under the bed by the window. "Don't you dare utter a sound," she threatened. She rolled her eyes before walking over the door and opening it. About ten ladies-in-waiting rushed in the room.

"Oh, Princess, has any harm come to you?" A soldier just arrived and reported to us that you were well outside of the border holding hands with a boy you claimed to be your fiancé. What in the world happened? You know you aren't allowed to leave the castle after midnight, much less the city borders. And who is the "fiancé" you were talking about?" One of the ladies-in-waiting who seemed to be in charge looked anxiously at the girl, fretted about nervously.

"Such lies! I was sleeping quite soundly until you, Esme, barged in with a group of people telling me a far-fetched story of me being outside the city borders with a boy that's supposed to be my fiancé, while I've been asleep in this bed the whole time!" The girl said indignantly. She had managed to look bleary eyed, and stifled a yawn.

"But, Princess, the soldier really said...." Esme began to say, but was interrupted by the girl. "Seriously, Esme, who would you believe, me or the silly soldier?"

"You, of course, Princess."

"Well then, you should know better than to believe those false rumors. Punish the soldier for me. Send him to the farthest part of the city for a month. You are now all dismissed." The girl said, with a nod to the rest of the ladies-in-waiting. They all turned in unison, and walked out of the door.

The girl listened at the closed door for a minute, let out a huge breath, then ran over to the bed and yanked Ryan out.

"Oww! Did you have to pull that hard?" Ryan asked.

"Now. Speak. Who are you? Why are you here? How did you get that box? Most of all, how did you know where my secret hideout was?" The girl's blue eyes seemed to pierce into Ryan's mind as she glared at him.

"Um, like I said. I have no idea why I got here; much less know that the field was your secret hideout. As for this," he produced the box from his pocket, "I was sleeping and it was on top of my bed when I woke up."

"Nonsense. That couldn't have happened," the girl declared.

"It's really true. When I touched this box, a purple hole appeared in my floor and led me to your field. Oh, yeah, my name is Ryan."

The girl studied him for a while, finally saying, "I don't see any way that could be possible, unless..." she gasped. "You're the...No, that can't be, but I'll take you to Cee anyway...." The girl seemed to be talking to herself instead of Ryan.

"What? You're gonna take me to see what? And now that I've introduced myself, it's supposed to be your turn, right?" Ryan was thoroughly confused.

The girl just sighed, "I guess I can wait till tomorrow to be sure of the truth. I am the princess of Daske, as you already know by now."

Ryan's eyes flitted to a framed photo of a younger version of the girl on her bureau. The caption underneath read, Jessica, age 8. "Your name is Jessica?" He asked.

"Why do people always pronounce it wrong? I am Princess Jessica. Say it after me. Je-SEE-ca."

"Je-SEE-ca." Despite the regal air Jessica had, Ryan couldn't help feeling drawn to her. She had a kind of flair that made him attracted to her already. Too bad she isn't any nicer, Ryan thought as Jessica said, "Tomorrow I will take you to Cee. Not see as in to watch something, but Cee spelled C-e-e. He's the court magician. You can hide in my room tonight in that corner." Without another word, she climbed onto her bed and pulled up the covers, ignoring Ryan completely.

He went to the corner and lay down on the floor. Just before he drifted off, he yawned and wondered who the heck Cee was, and what else the next day would bring.

"Get up. Now." Someone was kicking Ryan's feet. He opened his eyes and saw Jessica bending over him, holding a glass of milk and a plate of croissants in her hands. A person, who Ryan highly suspected was Jessica, had stuffed a pillow under his head and thrown a blanket roughly over him.

"Eat quickly. Later I'll take you to find out why you're here," Jessica said, setting the plate and milk on the floor beside him.

After a quick breakfast, Jessica made Ryan hide again, and called to Esme, her lead lady-in-waiting.

"I am going to the court magician's today. No one should be allowed to disturb us."

"Yes, Princess. I shall notice the staff immediately."

"Come, we have to hurry." Jessica took Ryan's hand, and they started to walk faster, almost running. They had slipped out of the castle using the rope again, and were now on their way to Cee's, whoever he was, house.

"Who is this guy, exactly?" Ryan asked as he hurried to match Jessica's quick-stepped paces.

"He is our city's most trusted advisor, and also actually one of my mentors in magic. Now stop talking. We're almost there." Jessica said.

They arrived at a white house. It was quite grand, but was still nothing compared to the castle. A man in an elaborate embroidered white robe was standing in front of the door.

"Greetings, I have been waiting for you. My name is Cee," the man said.

"What are you saying that you've been waiting for us? Does that mean you know about him already?" Jessica said curiously, pointing at Ryan beside her.

"Oh, yes, I've kept an eye on him for quite a while, and lately I've been given a sign that it was time, so I sent him the box and brought him here."

"YOU gave him the box? Then that means that—"

"Can you two stop talking about me like I'm not here?" Ryan interrupted, "And what do you mean that you have been spying on me for a while now?"

"I wouldn't call that spying," Cee replied airily, "that is what I call 'watching over'."

Ryan couldn't believe it. In a matter of hours, he had been whisked into another world, kidnapped by a princess, and now told by a strange man that he had been spied on for a period of time. That was way too much for him to handle.

"I don't care what you call it!" Ryan spat, "What did you bring me here for? I am perfectly happy with my life, thank you very much. Now take me home!"

"We're merely going to see if you're the right person," Cee said calmly.

"And what if I'm not?" asked Ryan.

An awkward silence filled the room.

"I suggest you not to know," Cee said with a dismissive wave of his hand. "It doesn't matter in your situation. You are most definitely the one we're searching for. We will start tomorrow. Accompany our guest to the west wing." The two guards behind him nodded and motioned Ryan to follow. Jessica trailed behind, apparently lost in her own thoughts.

They passed numerous statues and extravagant paintings before finally stopping in front of an intimidating stone arch. Although it was daytime, the interior was still quite dark, with only a small stream of sunlight coming from the windows high above. They kept walking until it was clear that the narrow path was a dead end.

One of the guards stepped toward and pushed a brick located at the left bottom side of the wall. There was a rumbling sound, but the wall still remained before them. The guard took a step forward, and just as Ryan was about to follow, an arrow whisked past him, narrowly missing his head.

With a strangled yelp he stumbled backwards. His cry caused the guards to turn, and he watched, mouth wide open, as the arrows passed harmlessly through their bodies.

"It's just an illusion designed to give the new recruited soldiers a scare. The wall is now an illusion as well," one guard assured him with a light chuckle.

It was kind of unsettling to see his own body come out of a wall, but Ryan couldn't help but wish he had bought a camera with him.

The room behind the wall was large, but it was cramped with weapons. There were rows of neatly lined swords, daggers, maces, clubs, spears, slingshots, and crossbows. Ryan also noticed a number of shields and helmets. However, what really attracted his attention was a tall glass case in the center of the room.

There was a single sword placed in it. It was silvery white, and the tip sparkled under the light of the guard's torches. The middle of the blade seemed to be transparent like glass, with silver streams of light flowing through it. The whole sword was sleek and elegant.

"Feel free to choose whatever weapon you like for tomorrow. I suggest you to choose a dagger, for they are lighter and easier to carry," one of the guards advised.

"What about this one?" Ryan asked, pointing at the white sword.

The two guards shared a look. "Well, that particular sword-"

"Is not something you want to handle. That is, if you actually *can* handle it," Jessica said with a smile. "Besides, sword craft is pretty hard to master."

"But you use a sw—"

"Here! Use this one. This dagger should be just right for you," Jessica said, purposely stopping his sentence and giving him a glare. She leaned closer and whispered into his ear, "Don't you dare mention me practicing in my hideout! Besides, I was only trying to enhance the sword with magic. Now take this dagger!"

Ryan felt his cheeks heat up due to their close proximity. Grudgingly he took the short knife from her hands. It was plain, but at least it was sharp and polished. He waved it experimentally.

They left the room after he chose the dagger.

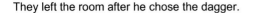

A man wearing a black embroidered cloak was standing silently before the window. He had one hand on the window pane and was staring intently at the boy and girl at the garden three stories below. The girl was constantly shaking her head as the boy made mistake after mistake. Finally, the boy did a right move, earning a relieved high five from the girl.

The windows remained open, but the person who opened them was nowhere to be found.

"One right move out of twenty-one wrong ones," Jessica announced, "Well, I wouldn't exactly call you hopeless, but this is pretty depressing."

Ryan gave a weak chuckle.

They had been practicing in the castle's garden for a while now. The sun was setting, casting a warm orange glow on everything else, but a low rumble from the distance signaled an oncoming storm, so the pair had to give up on improving Ryan's awful skills.

On his own defense, Ryan has to admit that he hasn't been paying much attention when Jessica was demonstrating him how to dodge and attack with a dagger, since his mind kept drifting back to the sleek white sword in its glass case.

"Ouch!" he suddenly cried out, rubbing his sore forehead, for Jessica had just smacked him. "What did you do that for?"

"That's for spacing out when I'm speaking. Well, if you really insist on skipping dinner, I guess I can tell the chef that I'd be dining alone."

"There's food? Awesome! Race ya!"

The two of them were panting when they finally got to the dining room back at the castle. The head chef was already waiting there with a list of dishes.

Jessica sat down at the head of the table, pointing at the menu the chef presented. The chef then nodded and left the room.

Which left Ryan staring awkwardly at the long oak table with nineteen vacant seats.

"Take your pick," Jessica said, eyes downcast, "it's not like anybody else would be coming."

Ryan hesitated, then settled down at the seat next to her. She was twirling her hair, pretending to be busy.

"I don't really have parents," he suddenly said, his voice echoing around the spacious room.

Jessica looked up, eyebrows raised, disappearing into her bangs.

"Um, I mean that I have parents."

Her mouth formed into a frown.

"Er, but they're hardly there so it feels like they're not there. Well, sometimes they *are* there but most of the time they're not so it feels like they're not there. And even though they sometimes come back they just stay for a day or so then they're off to somewhere else so it feels like—"

"They're not there," Jessica finished with a small smile. "I'm fine. I don't really remember what they look like anyway. They…passed away when I was six, and the city council handles the city pretty well. When I turn sixteen in two years, I shall be taking on the responsibility," She smiled wistfully, and Ryan suddenly found himself lost in her clear blue eyes.

A knock on the door broke the moment.

"The court magician is here," a servant announced.

"Bring him in," Jessica said.

Cee walked in, his long white robe trailing behind. "I see that the boy is here. Good. I am here to inform you that you will be given a task tomorrow. Come to me when you're finished with dinner and I will lead you to your room. Enjoy the food." He bowed low to Jessica and exited the room just as the servants came in with delicious looking appetizers.

Dinner was excellent and over in the blink of an eye. With the help of a servant, Ryan found Cee's house without any problem. When he arrived, he was led to Cee's study.

After twenty minutes of waiting, there was still no sign of Cee. Bored, Ryan decided to check out his surroundings. The whole place was neat and clean. There were no scattered papers or random piles of books, just an ancient looking desk at the back of the room and floor-to-ceiling bookshelves covering two walls. In short, it was boring and lifeless.

However, there was a large painting behind the wooden desk that looked oddly familiar to Ryan. It was a picture of a...microwave.

Why was there a picture of a microwave in another world? As far as Ryan knew, there was no technology in Daske. He walked over and placed a hand on the painting.

And fell headfirst into it.

There was a sound of the door opening, and when Ryan frantically looked up, he could see Cee coming in, followed by the servant who brought him there. Without thinking, he rushed into the giant microwave, slamming the door behind him.

The interior was dark; it was a microwave after all. Although a bit muffled, he could hear Cee and the servant talking.

"Are you sure he came in?" It was Cee speaking.

"Yes, master. I personally led the boy in half an hour ago," the servant answered.

"Did he, by any chance, slip out?"

"There were no reports of him leaving. Do you wish me to ask the patrols then, sir?"

"I will ask them myself. Excused."

There was the sound of the door opening again, and the sound of it closing.

Relieved, Ryan let out a breath and pushed the door. It didn't open. A new wave of panic washed through him, even more so when the disk he was crouching on began to rotate. The heat was rising quickly, and the disk was spinning even faster now. It was like getting on a roller coaster, except that he felt no exhilaration, only the stickiness of his own sweat, which only made him want to throw up even more.

Just when he thought he was about to lose it, the microwave stopped. The door flew open, and through his unfocused eyes, he could see Cee standing outside the painting, facing him.

His expression wasn't happy.

But his frown was quickly replaced by a smile while Ryan got out the painting, like it was never there in the first place.

"Follow me. I'll take you to your room." he simply said.

Ryan, on the other hand, wasn't quite sure why he was off the hook, but he wasn't about to complain. They finally got to his room, which was located on the east wing.

Cee shot him a calculating look, and then walked away.

The windows were closed now. Moonlight peeked in through a slot between the heavy curtains. The man in a black embroidered robe smiled as he read a piece of paper under the candlelight.

"Traitors will be unmasked," he seemed to murmur. "I wonder how soon that will happen."

The words on the paper were etched in his mind, forcing him to rethink them over and over. Two in particular stood out like a headline, so mesmerizing yet so annoying.

He scowled and tossed the piece of paper into the fireplace. Gradually the flames engulfed the paper, burning it into ashes.

Ryan was suddenly awake. Which was weird, since he could sleep through just about anything.

Something was calling him.

The uncanny feeling jerked him awake. Immediately he sat up in full alert.

Outside, the rain was falling nonstop. Almost as if in a trance, Ryan got up, put on a pair of slippers, and headed towards the door, seeking out whatever causing the mysterious feeling.

As he stepped out into the hallway, it was dark, the only source of light coming from torches randomly lit on the walls. Ryan could barely discern the silhouette of his hand as he waved it in front of him. He considered going back to his warm bed, when he felt the weird sensation again, that tugging feeling inside his heart. The decision was made for him. Ryan started down the hallway, determined to find out whatever it was.

Even though he didn't have enough time to get his bearings around the castle straight yet, Ryan found himself navigating the hallways without any problem. Whenever he faced a fork in the halls, he concentrated. Deep inside his mind, he felt the feeling telling him the right way to go. Without a specific destination in his mind, Ryan relied on his instincts, trusting whatever his heart said. About thirty minutes later, he found himself standing at the west wing where the weaponry room was.

Ryan remembered that a brick was pushed to reveal the hidden doorway, but which one? The only way was to push each brick. He started from the right, slowly working his way to the left, from bottom to top. Luckily, he didn't have to try for long. After he touched the fifth brick from the left on the third layer, the arrow shot past him. He wasn't fooled by the trick anymore, however, and tentatively stepped into the room.

The moment he entered, he was drawn but the glimmering sword displayed in the glass case. In the dark, the sword gave off a silver sheen like moonlight. At that instant, Ryan knew that it was what had been calling to him all that time. Entranced, Ryan stepped towards the sword, wishing to get a closer look. He put one hand on the glass case, admiring the silver streams of light inside the blade, forming different patterns like a kaleidoscope. To his surprise, the glass case was unlocked, allowing him to take out the silver sword. The very moment he touched it, the sword emitted a dazzling white glow, and that was the last thing he remembered before he passed out.

In his dream, everything was surrounded by a brilliant white glare. Ryan was inside a room full of people, but he didn't recognize a single face. A sudden flash of red caught his eye. A glamorous woman, probably in her late twenties, stepped into the center of the room. Her long blond hair swished side to side as she surveyed the room with piercing jade green eyes. One of her eyes was covered with a black eye patch and she was dressed in a dark red satin gown. In her hand was a blood-stained dagger with a black handle.

In a flash, so fast that Ryan didn't have the time to react, the woman stormed towards a person, and without hesitating, sliced his head straight off. Ryan opened his mouth to cry out for help, but his voice was stuck in his throat; not a single sound came out.

The woman walked back to the center of the room, and eyes focused on another prey, leaped towards the person who was shivering in fear, eyes pleading for mercy. This time, she plunged her dagger straight into the brain. The victim collapsed, still writhing on the floor.

It was like watching a horror movie, so terrifying yet fascinating. Ryan stared, transfixed, as he was unable to take his eyes off the beautiful assassin. As she slowly took away the lives of more and more people, each person killed in a different way, Ryan found himself staring awestruck at her actions.

She was like a ballerina prancing gracefully around the room; the only thing out of place was the killing involved with the choreography. The movements would have been elegant if the scene just wasn't so bloody.

The woman slashed another victim on the stomach, leaving blood oozing out of the gash. Ryan turned away, unable to face the sight of so much blood, when he felt someone staring at him. He looked up and saw the woman, her eye trained on him, walking towards his direction. He tried to run, but he found himself paralyzed, and could not move a single inch.

She was getting closer, a sadistic smile on her face.

Ryan could only stare at her, terrified, as the sharp blade came in contact with his throat.

Chapter 2

When Ryan finally regained his senses, he opened his eyes and saw a looming figure leaning over him. He tried to run, but he was lying on top of a cot and he was too weak anyway. "Stay put! Don't worry, you're safe now. We are in the castle infirmary," said a voice that was vaguely familiar. Ryan looked up, searching for the source of the voice, but only saw two blurry figures above him. When his vision finally cleared, he saw Cee and Jessica standing over him.

"What happened? I thought I saw a woman in a red dress, then I think I died or something. The agony was too much to bear......" His voice trailed off, leaving a worried look on his face.

"A woman in a red dress?" Cee asked. "Did she happen to have blond hair and a black eye patch?"

Ryan nodded. "She was killing people in a room, and even worse, she looked like she was enjoying it." He shuddered as he remembered the smile on her face when she walked towards him.

"May I see the sword?" Cee asked.

Ryan glanced down to see a silver sword clutched tightly in his hand. It was the sword in the weaponry room. Wordlessly he handed it to Cee.

Once it was in Cee's hands, the silver-white glow that was enveloping it disappeared. He handed it back to Ryan.

"Why is this sword especially in the glass case?" Ryan asked.

"This is the forbidden sword of light, destroyer of darkness and despair—Mirroride," Cee answered.

"Then why did I feel it calling to me if it is forbidden?"

Cee narrowed his eyes slightly when Ryan asked the question, and paused for a moment before replying, "The sword chooses the person to claim it. Since you felt it summoning you, we can only believe it has chosen you."

"Wait. Hold on a sec. Whaddaya mean it chose me?" Ryan was so amazed that his words came out in a jumble.

"The sword chooses its master. Mirroride's past owners all have had the same qualities. Courage. Wisdom. Confidence."

"You're saying that I have all those qualities?" Ryan asked incredulously, for the Ryan he knew usually did silly things like licking batteries, which in his opinion, wasn't either brave or wise.

Cee's face was expressionless.

"The woman you saw is Cynthiana Lorahas, leader of the notorious group E.Y.E., which stands for 'Exile You for Eternity'. She, for reasons unknown, will stop at nothing to kill the people in Daske."

"Exile you for eternity? Give me a break," Ryan said incredulously. "That name sounds far too stupid for an assasin group."

"That group with the stupid name wiped out Darke, a strong neighbor of us with a population of twenty-four million people, and burned down the whole city, " said Cee.

"Whoa, wait a second. You're saying that this lady is planning to wipe out Daske too? I'm getting outta here," declared Ryan.

"You can't leave!" blurted Jessica. Cee shot her a warning look.

"I'm not part of this world. You'll have to deal with the group yourself," said Ryan.

Cee lowered his head, and then said, "Follow me, then. I'll show you why you need to be here. May you excuse us for a moment, Princess?"

He led Ryan out of the room to a three-way hallway and walked straight to the middle one.

"This, is the prophecy room," Cee said, pointing forwards a golden double door carved with an elegant D. He pushed open the doors and Ryan found himself looking at the most glamorous room in his life.

The room was so large that three stadiums could fit into it with room to spare, and the decorations took Ryan's breath away. There were lavender curtains and midnight blue drapings everywhere. Floating in the middle of the room was a glowing orb the size of a basketball. It was giving off the same eerie purple light as the portal Ryan saw in his room a few days ago.

"What that?" Ryan asked, pointing to the orb.

"The very thing that keeps the EYE from destroying us. It contains powerful magic and allows protection," said Cee.

"Then why are you guys so afraid of them?"

"They'll eventually find a way to get in. Cynthiana has been known for her incredible patience and strategy skills."

"Okay..." Ryan couldn't think of anything to cheer them up.

"Anyhow, that is not your concern. Look at the walls."

Ryan looked up, and saw words engraved on every bit of the four walls, ceiling, and even some parts of the floor.

"What are they?" Ryan asked.

"Prophecies. Some had happened; others we're still waiting. Come, I'll show you the prophecy you were foreseen in."

Ryan followed Cee to the wall in front of them and Cee pointed to one on the middle.

A warrior of Earth shall come to Daske
Destroy the E.Y.E., traitors unmask
With luck, the things he seek release
To their rightful owner, the truths unleash.

"What's that supposed to mean?" Ryan asked.

"It means that you're the one who's going to destroy Cynthiana." Cee answered.

"ME?! No, no, no, you've got the wrong person"

Cee stopped, and then he took a deep breath. "I am sorry to inform you this, but if you do not wish to help us, you are no use to us in the city. What would you prefer to be, a useless boy wandering in the streets of Daske, or the big hero that saved a city? Besides, we do not know when the next portal to your world will appear."

The tiniest smirk appeared on his face. He knew that Ryan didn't have a choice. Ryan realized that Cee had planned this all along, and that was the reason why he had excluded Jessica while explaining the situation.

"I don't have a choice, do I?"

"Glad that you realized. Do you have the black box?"

Ryan nodded.

"It is made of Kelsian Obsidian, which, with our resources, is unable to open unless we have a special key. The key can't be copied because the keyhole changes shape whenever the wrong key is inside it. The box can't be penetrated. Only the original key made to match this box can open it."

"Do you know who has the key, then?" Ryan knew that he would be sent to find the key, so he kept repeating in his mind: Please not with Cynthiana, please not with Cynthiana...... However, his fears were confirmed. "The key has been lost for a long time. Rumor has that it is now a belonging of the EYE, and you are to retrieve it. I'm sorry we don't have enough time to train you properly, but what we have done is enough. You will start tomorrow." Cee said seriously, "Here is a charm to remind you of your goal on this quest." He handed Ryan a small key. "Consider it a good luck charm." Cee smiled then walked away, leaving Ryan alone in the prophecy room.

"You did an excellent job." said Cynthiana as she painted her fingernails red with slow, even strokes.

"Anything for you, darling. Anything," purred a man in black.

"Well, when I first saw that idiotic prophecy, I thought the 'warrior' was going to be a grown man, but I suppose him being only a boy might work to our advantage."

"He may look stupid, but his energy flows differently than us."

"I don't care. But I'll send Ivy and Travix to distract Ryan and Jessica. Now get out of here."

"As you say, my dear."

Ryan sighed as he placed a set of clothes in his backpack. They were leaving tomorrow and he just couldn't seem to fall asleep. He knew his parents won't even notice that he was gone. They were too busy working anyway. There was another thing that was bothering him. One minute he was just walking down the street wondering whether he should buy a mint-choc ice-cream or a fruit smoothie, and the next minute he was whisked away to a magical kingdom and practically being forced to become their warrior. That was way too much for a fourteen-year-old. At least on the plus side, Jessica was going with him. After adding another bar of chocolate in his pack, he finally fell asleep.

In his dream, Ryan saw a cow. He was terrified to death around cows since one ate his pants and underwear in kindergarten. Now, no matter who tried to convince him, he still believed that cows are vicious killers that love to eat pants. However, this cow he saw was even scarier. It was ten feet tall, bright red, and had sharp horns that were jet black. The thing that freaked him out the most wasn't the cow, surprisingly. The cow had a black velvet blanket with the symbol of E.Y.E., a large eye with a blood red iris, on it, and sitting on top of the cow, was Cynthiana. She looked right into Ryan's eyes, and said, "Come, little warrior, we know your greatest fear. Daisy here will always be waiting for you."

Ryan woke up with a start. Jessica was shaking him. She was already dressed in a long white sleeveless top and tight black pants, prepared to set off on their journey. "What did you mean 'No Cows'? You kept repeating that again and again when you were asleep."

"Er... You must have imagined it," Ryan said lamely. Jessica raised an eyebrow.

"Whatever. We're leaving now, so you might as well get some breakfast. It's going to be a long journey," said Jessica.

"The brats have set off for their ridiculous quest," the man in black reported to Cynthiana.

"Excellent. According to our plan, when they reach Taske, Ivy and Travix will be able to you them and report back information. Aren't I brilliant? Oooh, it's time for my massage!"

Ryan sat down a stone beside the road. "Are we there yet?" he complained.

"Can't you stop asking me? I answered this question five seconds ago. No!" snapped Jessica.

A whole day of walking under the burning sun had boiled Jessica's patience and good temper, and with Ryan complaining every five seconds wasn't helping at all. They were heading towards Taske, which she hadn't visited before, but Cee assured that it was perfectly safe.

"How far is it, then?" asked Ryan. In answer, Jessica pointed forward. He could just make out a tiny tip of a building behind the trees. Great, he thought, I'm done walking. He shook the water bottle; it made a hollow whooshing sound. "I'll go make a refill," he said, pointing to the nearby river.

"No, I'll go," said Jessica, "the last time you did it, you ended up losing a water bottle."

"The water was way to fast!" Ryan protested.

"Yeah, of course," she retorted.

"Fine. You go," he said. Jessica stomped away without a word. He was just making himself comfortable on the grass when he heard a high-pitched scream.

"HELP! HELP! THERE'S A BEAR!"

He dashed into the forest, searching for the source of the voice. The person screaming didn't sound like Jessica at all, so he ran deeper in, following the sound of the voice. Finally he found a girl and a by perched on top of a tree, desperately trying to avoid the razor-sharp claws of a clearly angered bear.

It noticed Ryan and charged him instead. Just as the bear was about to claw him in the face, Ryan pulled Mirroride out of his scabbard, held it in front of him, and closed his eyes, preparing for the worst. When he was sure he was about to die, he heard the bear howl in agony. He opened his eyes, and was surprised to see the bear sprawled on the ground struggling for the last moments of its life. Ryan looked around to see who had killed the bear, but a flash of light on the bear's stomach caught his eye. He saw Mirroride's blade embedded in the bear, and when he pulled it out, the blade was coated red. Ryan realized that he had killed the bear. He killed a wild living thing for the first time. Normally, it would have made him totally excited, but as he looked at the bear's carcass, he felt only one emotion: regret. He had killed a living thing to protect himself, but he still didn't like it.

"Thank you for saving us. I don't have anything valuable," the girl started to say, but she was interrupted by Jessica's sharp. "Ryan! If you're not here within ten seconds, I'm leaving without you."

"Sorry, I gotta go," Ryan told them.

"We are very grateful for your help," the boy said. "I'm sure that we will meet again soon."

"Bye!" Giving them one last wave, Ryan raced off for find Jessica.

The boy nimbly got off the tree then gently helped the girl down. Their platinum blond hair sparkled under the soft sunlight passing through the leaves above them. The boy took out an azure wand and with a quick wave, the dead bear disappeared.

"It's him. Let's go," he told the girl with a smile.

She was waiting at the spot where they separated. Jessica looked at Ryan's face, and then at Mirroride's blade, which was covered in blood.

"What happened? Do you know how worried I was about you? Can't you ever stop getting into trouble?" Jessica was so mad that she kept stumbling over her words and she looked like she was about to have a fit.

"I'm sorry Jess, but guess what happened!" Ryan said. He told Jessica about his encounter with the bear, and her eyes got wider with every sentence. When he was finished, she exclaimed, "How could you be so stupid? Normal people don't usually carry swords with them. By showing the kids Mirroride, it's like telling them about Daske!"

"Yeah, I shouldn't have pulled the sword out, but what was weird was that the kids didn't seem surprised about Mirroride, as if they were expecting it." Ryan looked at his sword fondly, but then gasped out loud, "All the blood's gone!"

Jessica narrowed her eyes. "Who were they? What did they look like?"

"Well... I didn't really take a good look at the boy, because he was pretty much hidden behind leaves and branches, but the girl was..." Ryan had a dreamy expression on his face.

"The girl was what?" Jessica had a bad feeling about what Ryan was going to say.

"The girl was seriously pretty. I mean, I've never seen anyone like that! Is silvery-blond hair and violet eyes common in this world?"

Jessica looked thoughtful. "I don't know. People are mostly brunettes here." She snuck one look at Ryan's hair, and turned a bit red.

"But, anyway, maybe she is wearing contacts, you dork," she muttered. "The blood might have just been a mirage. We'll need to be careful as we go along. Now, stop daydreaming about that girl!"

"I'm not daydreaming!" protested Ryan.

"Yeah, right," she said sarcastically. "Well, let's just ignore that for now." They set off down the road, when Ryan felt something tugging at his shoulder.

"Hey, cut it out!" He yelled, but instead of stopping, the tugging became more intense. Then, a wet handkerchief with a weird smell was pressed upon his face. At the same time, Ryan heard Jessica scream in terror. The handkerchief must have been soaked in narcotics, since Jessica's scream was the last thing he heard before he blacked out.

Ryan woke up in a dark room, and since he couldn't see anything, he could only guess that the lump beside him was Jessica. He squinted his eyes and saw two other lumps across the room. He immediately tensed, and reflexively clutched Mirroride, which was miraculously still on his leather belt. As he started to get up, he found out that his left ankle was chained to Jessica's with a metal chain that was as thick as a baby's arm.

"Ryan, Ryan!" Jessica hissed by his ear, "Where are we?"

"I don't know. I only got up about three minutes before you."

"You should've been more careful!"

"I'm sorry. But you weren't much better either."

"Unlock."

"Pa.. Pardon?"

"Not you, dummy. This lock," Jessica pointed at the chain, which now fell on the floor.

"Oh, right. I forgot you can do magic! Awesome!" Ryan said.

Jessica turned bright red, and then said, "It's nothing... I'm only a Ruby, so I can't perform complicated magic, but I'll be a Sapphire soon."

"What Sapphire?" Ryan asked.

"There are five levels of magic. Amethyst, emerald, ruby, sapphire, diamond. See this necklace?" She showed her necklace to Ryan, "it's a dark red ruby. Each level has three ranks: Light, clear, and dark. Cynthiana's a light Diamond, by the way."

23

Just as Jessica finished her sentence, the two lumps across the room started to struggle. Ryan immediately went into battle mode, unsheathing his sword and thrusting it in front of him. Jessica pulled out a crimson wand and started muttering under her breath. When they both were prepared for the attack, one of the lumps spoke.

"Travix, have you any idea where we be?" asked a girl's voice.

"You can talk?!" Ryan said incredulously.

"Yes. Who are you? Do you know how we can get away?" This time it was a boy who spoke.

Ryan slowly walked towards them, and then he let out a gasp, "You... You guys are the two kids trapped on the tree!"

"Hey! We be fourteen!" protested the girl, who had stormed out of their previous corner the instant Ryan said "kid".

"You speak weird," said Ryan.

"It's just the way she talks. You'd get used to it," said the boy, emerging from the dark.

Under the dim light, Ryan could vaguely make out a boy wearing a midnight blue hooded cape over a black shirt and trousers. His hand was clutched by a girl in a lavender dress that fell to her knees. They both had light blond hair like strands of silver and violent eyes, only the boy's were a shade darker. One look at them told Ryan that they were twins.

"I am Travix, and this is my sister Ivinia, Ivy for short."

Jessica stormed forward, her ice blue eyes flashing angrily, "What are you two up to? Ryan saves your pitiful lives, and then we get kidnapped? This must have something to do with you."

"Trust me. I have absolutely no idea where we are. If I really want to kidnap you, wouldn't it be suspicious that we did it after you just met us?" Travix said calmly.

"I still don't believe you," said Jessica with scowl.

"It doesn't matter," then he took in Jessica's necklace, "You can also perform magic? Excellent. Now I don't have to hide mine." He pulled out a pendant with thin black metal chains and a light blue sapphire in the middle.

"Who did you train with?" Jessica asked. Travix started to answer, and then stopped.

"We are sworn under circumstances that we will never tell anyone who our leader is," he answered. "However, since we are together now, why don't we travel together along the way? You two seem to be on a quest or some kind of trip. Ivy and I are also on a mission too. If we work together, we would be much more efficient."

"Give us some time to discuss," Jessica said, pulling Ryan into a corner. After a heated discussion, they accepted. Then, with Travix and Jessica working their magic, and Ryan hacking the door with Mirroride, they finally managed to escape.

Chapter 3

"I still don't trust them," whispered Jessica as they walked towards Taske. Travix and Ivy followed quietly behind them, occasionally exchanging words.

"Why not?" asked Ryan.

"Don't you think it's a little weird for us to get kidnapped with them and then get out of that black room that easily?"

"You guys seemed to be pretty good at magic."

"It's strange, though. I can break a simple lock spell without any problem, but I couldn't unlock that room. And when Travix came over to help me, he blasted the whole roof off with a single flick of wrist."

"He's level is higher than you."

Jessica shook her head, puzzled. "One level isn't much different. He must be a higher rank than light Sapphire."

"Okay. Okay. We won't say anything about our quest, and when something dangerous happens, we ditch them," said Ryan, throwing his hands up.

"Be you really going to report them to Cynthiana, Travix? They seem nice." Ivy said to Travix, her huge violet eyes filled with worry.

"Cynthiana seemed pretty nice at as when she adopted us too, and look who she turned out to be," muttered Travix. "You are too soft, sister. Soft hearts cannot survive in the cruel reality. Besides, I don't think they trust us either. Jessica is already suspicious about my level. That distraction spell isn't going to work forever."

"But I still think that this is wrong. Maybe we can help them and be friends, please?"

"Stop whining! I am older than you and you shall do what I say. Now, report to Cynthiana."

"We are twins! You be only ten minutes older than me!"

"Be quiet! Or Ryan and Jessica are going to find out about us any second. Contact Cynthiana or I'll take away Goldie."

Ivy paled. Goldenflight was her favorite bow. With Goldie, as she nicknamed it. Ivy never failed to short anything she set her eyes on. The thought of taking away Goldie made Ivy tremble with fear, so she took out a small piece of paper with the EYE symbol on it and scribbled down a few words. With a wave of his wand, Travix made the message disappear and sent it on its way.

"Yes!" Cynthiana exclaimed as she lay back on her leather recliner, looking her huge plasma screen.

"What makes you so excited, dear?" asked the man in black.

"Travix and Ivy have teamed up with the two brats, and are accompanying them on their silly quest. As you know, my favorite saying is: Keep your friends close, but your enemies closer. Now, Ivy and Travix are able to report Ryan and Jessica's moves every minute! Isn't this great?"

"If you are happy, I am too, sweetheart."

"Don't call me sweetheart! Now off to your work!"

"Yes, of course. I'll go this second."

"Are there any cool monsters in Taske?" asked Ryan eagerly.

"I don't know. But we'll head to the market first. It's famous for selling water nymph melodies, dragon scales, and all kinds of magical objects," said Jessica.

"How do you sell a song? Are we going to watch a show in the market?"

"No, the melodies are captured inside a jar and when the jar is opened, something magical happens."

"What stuff?"

"It depends. Sometimes it explodes, turns everyone invisible, or even gives you superpowers, such as defying gravity or moving objects with your mind, for a while or so. A few of the right jars would be useful to have with us on the trip."

"Cool! What are the other magical objects?"

"You'll see."

27

They walked along the path, and then finally saw the huge golden gate of Taske. The instant they walked through, they were surrounded by a bunch of people.

"Good morning! We'll offer you a full introduction of Taske just for a few zarae. We'll tell you all kinds of information. You ask it, we answer it," the guides said in unison.

Ryan looked hopefully at Jessica. "We had a zarae or two to spare, right?"

Jessica sighed and said, "Alright, but..."

"We be rich. We can pay," interrupted Ivy, showing them a pouch full of coins. Travix shot her a look, but she simply shrugged.

"This is the market where we sell all sorts of magical objects. Feel free to look around!" Everywhere they saw, there were booths selling everything from flying brooms to rainbow-colored fruits and vegetables.

"Are those werewolf whiskers? Cool!" Ryan raced over to a stand, the others hurrying behind him.

"Werewolf whiskers are the best for tracking things. Attach the scent to the whiskers, and they will pull you toward the right direction. A bundle for twenty zarae! Best bargain you'll ever get!"

"Jess, can we buy this? Pretty puh-lease with a cherry on top?"

"We don't have the scent of what we're looking for, so this is practically useless to us," Jessica said. "Sorry, maybe next time," she said to the merchant.

"Hey! What about that? What's that?" Ryan asked, pointing to a row of glass bottles.

"That is Pranking Gas. Good for driving everyone crazy. I've heard that one boy turned his mother into a slug for a few weeks. Ten zarae per jar! Best bargain you'll ever get!"

"Don't even think about it," said Jessica.

"Aww... come on," Ryan pleaded.

"But we do need some Fruity Mixers," said Jessica.

"Fruity Mixers? That's a good choice. Follow me." The guides led them to another booth with bright, colorful fruits.

"Oooh, they be pretty!" said Ivy, looking at a star shaped fruit with an amazing shade of pink and purple.

"I'd like to have a sack," said Jessica.

"Alright, missy, that will be fifty zarae." Just as Jessica was about to pull out her purse, Ivy walked forward and said, "I'll pay for her."

"Ivy!" Travix almost shouted, but she ignored him and paid to it.

"Hey, what's that?" Ryan asked excitedly at Jessica. He was pointing at a greenish-yellow ball a boy was buying at the next booth.

"Eww, the color be gross!" said Ivy, scrunching her nose.

"That's a Color Splash. Nothing magical. Just a mixture of ogre snot, mustard, and mermaid tears," one of the tour guides said.

"What can it do?" asked Ryan.

"You just throw it towards someone and it explodes. The colors are never the same, and the smell, well, the smell is just plain nasty," one of the tour guides answered.

Ryan's eyes shined. Jessica knew he wanted to buy some, but it seemed to be useless.

"Only 5 zarae for 10 balls, it's the —"

"I know, I know. Best bargain you'll ever get," Jessica said, rolling her eyes. She started to say no, but stopped when Ryan stared at her expectantly with adorable puppy eyes.

"Alright!" She threw her hands up in surrender and handed the merchant the money.

"Thanks Jess," said Ryan as he gingerly picked up one of the balls. "It's slimy!" he dropped the ball and it bounced back to his hand. "And it bounces!"

"The smell be awful," Ivy pouted.

"Now, we're going to get some jars of water nymph melodies." Jessica said.

"Awesome! Can I pick out the jars?" Ryan asked.

"Fine, but the jars are unlabeled, so you'll get an even chance of picking out something cool or not."

The guides led Ryan and the others to the entrance of a dark alley and said, "Although Taske is widely known for the melodies, the merchants are actually banned from selling it because it caused plenty trouble before."

"What trouble?"

"The EYE used it as weapons and it caused a lot of mayhem."

Then they walked into the alley and stopped in front of an old rickety cottage with a table on its porch. What was breathtaking was that there were about twenty jars filled with bubbling air of luminous colors on top of the table. Every color imaginable was inside a different jar, from bright colors such as fuchsia and topaz, to darker tones such as jet black and chocolate brown.

All of them stood enthralled and watched the jars filled with the colored bubbling air until a raspy voice said, "One hundred zarae for a jar," and startled them out of their wits. They turned and saw an old man with white hair, and a long beard almost reaching his stomach, leaning on a cane in front of the door.

"The brighter colored jars usually give you superpowers, while the darker jars are mainly used for attack, such as exploding things."

"Is there anything for defense?" Travix asked, looking concerned. "Something that can defend diamond leveled magic."

The man thought for a moment and shrugged, "It depends on your luck. Defense powers aren't popular here."

Travix looked seriously at Ryan and asked, "May I pick?" Ryan nodded.

"Okay, follow me," the man said. The group started to follow, but then he added, "Only the one that chooses."

"What about these jars?" asked Jessica, pointing to the jars on the table.

"They're just decorations," he answered. Leading the way, Travix disappeared into the dark alley with him.

Travix and the man walked silently for a few moments, but then the man spoke.

"So you think you're quite clever, don't you? Thinking up that distraction spell?"

Travix stopped and stared at the man, speechless.

"Pardon me? A distraction spell? I have no idea what you mean."

"Stop pretending. I could see through that easy spell as soon as I saw you."

"But that spell is top secret! There are only two people in the world who know this spell. My teacher and I."

"Actually there is one more person. Have you ever thought of who invented that spell? I did. I made up that easy spell to trick people into thinking your magic level is lower than it really is, and I taught it to only one person. Cynthiana adopted you, right?"

Travix nodded, than said, "How did you know Cynthiana?"

"Oh, she was one of my brightest students about ten years ago. The most clever and witty girl you'll ever find. Too bad she became obsessed with black magic and went over to the bad side. Then she changed," he sighed and look up at the sky. "By the way, my name is Lucas. Magic level dark diamond," he said, holding up a silver pocket watch with a blackish jewel in the center of the lid.

"Dark diamond?! I thought no one ever reached that level," Travix said, shocked.

Lucas, the old man looked amused. "Perhaps that's because no one wants to let others know about their level, just like you and the distraction spell."

Travix's face reddened. "I only did that because Cynthiana told me to," he said defensively.

"Well, you shouldn't listen to Cynthiana anymore. Black magic is the only thing she can think of now."

"Can you help me destroy Cynthiana? Or at least make her become good?"

"It'll be hard, but I think I know who can help us. They might not be willing, but they're probably the only ones who know everything. Now quickly choose some jars. The others are probably impatient, having to wait such a long time."

Travix looked at the array of jars on the shelves. After a while, he selected five jars. One was orange with white swirls and yellow sparks, another one was periwinkle purple with translucent pink bubbles in it. Those two would probably give some of them superpowers. The ones for attack were midnight blue with black streaks that looked like it had golden clouds floating on top, and brown with white spots, which looked like a mug of hot chocolate with marsh mallows. The final one was the one Travix wasn't sure whether it gave superpowers or was for attack. It was pure silver and gave off a glow like moonlight.

Lucas gave him a bag, and he carefully placed the jars inside. "That would be five hundred zarae," he said. Travix paid him and said, "Um, well. Would you, you know, accompany us on our journey? I don't think those two are too reliable."

Lucas thought for a moment. "I find that Ryan boy interesting. He has an unnatural flow of energy. And of course I would like to know my former student's apprentices better." He smiled at him.

"So you'll come? Great!" said Travix, then he rushed out the alley to find the others.

"Need to fix my mistake," Lucas muttered to himself. "Can't let her turn him into another killing machine." Then he shook his head and followed the boy out.

When Travix and Lucas were picking out the jars, Ivy was having a hard time. Jessica kept pressing her about where they came from, why they were traveling, and especially who their mentor was.

"I can't tell you!" Ivy looked like she was on a verge of tears.

"Sure you can. Travix is not here," said Jessica.

Ryan, who was bored out of his skull with the conversation, said, "I'm going to check out the other shops." Even though it was almost night time, the streets were still packed with people. Each bright colored sign fascinated Ryan, the products ranging from unicorn horns to mermaid scales. He was so absorbed in the signs that he failed to see the old lady with a black hood in front of him and bumped into her.

"Watch it, young man," she said, coughing. "These old bones can't handle it anymore." Then she looked up Ryan and gasped.

"What? I'm sorry," said Ryan, as he helped her up.

"You're that warrior," the old lady blurted out and immediately covered her mouth.

"Warrior? What warrior? I'm no warrior," said Ryan, doing a really bad job trying to look innocent.

"Stop playing dumb," she said when she was sure Ryan isn't going to kill her for knowing it. "I'm a fortune teller. A very good one too, for your information. I saw your face in my Kuloo." She started rummaging in her bag and pulled out a dirty black bowl with a crack on the side. "When it's filled with werewolf saliva, which I was planning to buy before you bumped into me, I can see a little bit of the future."

"Awesome! Did you see anything else?" asked Ryan excitedly.

"No, only a picture of you," she said. "But I bet I'll see more when I get that saliva!" she added when she saw Ryan's disappointed expression.

Ivy was about to throw a temper tantrum if Jessica asked her one more question, when she saw Travix and the old man coming down the alley.

"Hi, Travix!" she called. Jessica immediately shut up about the questions.

"Everyone, this is Lucas, and he'll be coming with us on our trip. Oh, and come and see what jars I picked out." Travix opened the bag and held out the jars. Jessica and Ivy crowded in for a look, but something felt missing. Ryan wasn't jumping up and down and exclaiming about the jars. In fact, he wasn't there at all.

"Um, where's Ryan?" Travix asked, looking around. At the sound of Ryan's name, everyone turned and looked around, but he was nowhere in sight.

"Lemme see," Ryan begged when the lady poured the saliva into Kuloo.

"My Kuloo only works for me. If you looked into it, you would only see your reflection staring back." The woman told him.

After Kuloo was full of saliva, it started to swirl and the lady stared onto it for about a minute. Then, she closed her eyes and said, as if in a trance, "You will travel to the brightest cave. One of tour companions will experience agony, and the least likely choice will become your friend."

"Come on, that's so vague. Can't you say anything more specific?" Ryan said.

"The gift of seeing the future only lets you see parts of it. However, if you want specific, I can tell you something. Your partner actually has quite strong feelings for you. Such a lovely girl, isn't she?"

"You mean Jessica? No way!"

"Oh yes, anyway, I saw that I will accompany your group in the future, so we might as well go meet the others now."

When Ryan and the old lady arrived at the dark alley, everyone was waiting for them. The old lady, who had been chattering happily at first, became silent and glared at Lucas.

"Well, well, look who's here. The great, famous, stuck-up Evelynda the Fortune Teller. What are you here for?" Lucas asked. He didn't look too pleased about the new arrival.

"Very funny, Lucas," Evelynda replied. She gave Ryan a look that said, Are we really traveling with there kind of people?

"Wait a second. You two know each other? And, Ryan, why did this old woman come here with you?" Jessica looked confused.

"Oh, yes, young lady, Lucas and I go way back. We've been arguing for the past sixty years. As for why I'm here, I saw in the future, I will be traveling with you for the next few days, so we might as well begin now."

"You can really see the future?" Ivy asked, looking excited. "Will I be pretty when I grow up?"

"Ivy!" Travix scolded. "Now isn't the time to ask such things."

33

"Yes, Ivy, since you are quite lovely now, I imagine you'll still be as beautiful when you've grown up." Lucas interrupted. "Now, I know someone who might know the place of the things you seek. We will have to visit Cubi Crescent."

"No fair!" cried Evelynda. "You ruined all the fun. I wanted to be the one tell them."

"What the heck is Cubi Crescent?" Ryan asked.

"It is the largest dragon community near human civilization. It's not very far, and dragons have amazing powers, so they'll be able to help us, but they may not be willing. We'll need to be careful. Ha! I got to explain Cubi Crescent. I win, old man!" Evelynda smirked.

"Dragons? Cool! Finally something I'm interested in!" said Ryan.

"I'll lead the way," said Lucas.

"Get outta the way, you old geezer. You move as fast as a tortoise. By the time we get to the dragons, Ryan here would be as old as us," said Evelynda, shoving Lucas aside.

"I don't take orders from crazy old ladies," said Lucas with a huff.

"Who are you calling crazy? At least I don't walk with a cane!" she shot back.

"Um, sorry. But I suggest that Lucas here can lead the way, while you can explain Cubi Crescent more to us. Okay?" Ryan said to Evelynda.

"Sounds good to me. See? We who can see the future get to explain the important stuff, while old men with a stick hobble around moving at a speed of one foot per minute."

"Okay, OKAY! Stop arguing. Let's get going." Jessica burst out. So they went.

Chapter 4

After two whole days of walking, they finally arrived in front of a group of huge rocks, the smallest one as tall as a six-story building. Evelynda proved to be really helpful, always gathering of odd plants and mushrooms to cook meals for them. "See, that's the reason why we take experienced fortune tellers on trips, not cranky old wizards," she said.

"Let's see how you can defend yourself when you're attacked by cranky old wizards," Lucas always retorted, then chased her around, trying to zap her with electricity.

There was a cave formed by the rocks, and when the group approached it, they could see lots of lights coming out of it, and felt quite hot. However, the most astonishing thing was a dark green dragon with blue markings standing in front of the entrance. When it saw them, it waved and said cheerily, "Hello! Welcome to the annual sports day of the Cubi Crescent dragon community. Humans are highly welcome here, but try not to get underfoot. Getting stepped on by a galumphing dragon by accident can be quite messy, and we'd need to fill in quite a lot of papers explaining the situation. I'd hate to see any of your tiny bodies in our death corner by the end of the day!"

"Knur! Knur! Take our guests to the king. And make sure to show them all the competitions!" he called out. A smallish dragon with fiery red scales emerged. He stared at them with his beautiful emerald green eyes.

"Yes, Zartar." The little dragon bowed how head respectfully. "Come with me, I'll take you to King Razi."

The dragons had certainly put in a lot of effort in decorating their cave. The floor was not made of rocks but a green grass carpet. The cave looked small from the outside, but there was a long, endless tunnel filled with glittering lights, and on one side, there was a sparking waterfall. Dragons of various colors were diving down and creating large splashes. Wherever they looked, dragons were either practicing or competing in all kinds of races, including Long Distance Fire Breathing, and Dragon Wrestling.

Ryan noticed Knur eyeing a sparkle she-dragon with silvery white scales that shined like star.

"She's pretty, isn't she? Why don't you invite her to go with us?" he asked.

"Oh, no, no, no. She's Keelia, Euricus's girlfriend. He'd scrape my scales off if I even dare to speak to her, "Knur answered, then pointed to a huge pure black dragon across the field, easily lifting a rock the size of a truck with one wing.

"Hey. Why aren't you in some competition? All the others are," said Ryan.

"Really. Tell me something that I'd be good at," said Knur.

"You'd be excellent at ...um, hide and seek?" Travix offered, trying to cheer him up.

"Seriously? Hide and seek?" Ryan deadpanned.

"I'm just trying to help," Travix muttered, turning a bit red.

"Anyway," Ryan said to Knur, "Why don't you give it a try?"

"Nah. I'd just make a fool out of myself. And even if I didn't, Euricus will do it for me," he said.

"You poor little thing, " said Ivy, wrapping her arms around him.

"I don't need any pity," said Knur, shrugging out of Ivy's hug. "Let's go see King Razi now."

King Razi didn't sit on a throne like normal kings. Instead, he was participating in the Waterfall Jump. Everyone watched him jump down and land with a tremendous splash. Everyone started to laugh, and when he surfaced, he laughed harder than anyone.

"King Razi is one of the best king we've ever had," said Knur. "He's nice to everyone, and doesn't act all high and mighty. Sometimes, he even has more fun than any of us when all the dragons are together." Knur led them to the king. King Razi had dark purple scales with platinum tips. However, his expression was cheerful and kind, not intimidating at all.

"Hi there, humans! Oh, it's you, Lucas and Evelynda. Still arguing every five seconds, I'd reckon," King Razi said in a cheerful voice.

"I've been here for five times, but it never fails to impress me," said Lucas, bowing to the king.

"Oh you know how much I hate those manners, come and join our festival!" he said.

"As much as I want to, we're actually here to seek information," said Evelynda, butting into the conversation.

"What information?" asked King Razi.

Evelynda pushed Ryan to the front. "Ask it," she said.

"Um, hi, my name is Ryan and uh, do you know where to find the key that matches this box?" he asked nervously.

The king lifted the box up with one wing and examined it closely. "Made of Kelsian Obsidian, huh? Pretty tricky stuff" He closed his eyes for a minute. "I've got it!"

"Thank you!" said Ryan, relieved.

"Not so fast, boy. I'll tell you where it is under one condition. You need to win at least one game," he said.

"You mean he has to compete with all the other gigantic dragons?" Evelynda exclaimed. "There's no way he could win!"

"Hey!" Ryan protested.

"Well, it's true," Evelynda said defensively.

"Don't get ahead of yourself. You can choose any dragon you want to assist you," King Razi said.

All the dragons stopped whatever they were doing and stared at Ryan. Well, every dragon except one.

"Knur," Ryan said aloud." I choose Knur," he repeated, more confident now.

"You must be kidding me," said a deep voice. It was Euricus.

"Why not? Knur's probably great at everything, only that you don't give him the chance to prove himself."

"Ryan, don't try to boost me up, I know you don't want me as a partner," Knur spoke up.

"Yeah, the little guy said so. Now, Ryan, choose me. Otherwise you'll ruin my record of being chosen every time," Euricus said, puffing out his chest.

"I said I choose Knur, and that's a final," Ryan snapped. Euricus looked both shocked and furious at the same time.

"Beware, human. Enjoy your day, 'cause this may be your last," Euricus snarled, then stormed away with his groupies.

"You shouldn't have done that," muttered Knur to Ryan.

"Someone has to show that boy that he doesn't rule the whole world," he replied.

"Okay then. Partner all chosen? You're about to compete in one of the most exciting dragon sports events ever. The Dragon Obstacle Course!" King Razi pointed to a darker part of the cave. There were jagged walls, numerous sharp stones floating around, and some creepy black clouds that Ryan couldn't identify.

"The first one who finds this," King Razi held his crown high up, "is the winner!" He threw the crown inside the cave, and it soon disappeared.

"Contestants please line up," the dragon that greeted them at the entrance, Zartar, announced.

"Hop on, "Knur said, "I think I can handle it. But don't blame me if I hit a wall."

"On your mark, get set, GO" King Razi shouted.

The second King Razi said "Go!" Euricus opened his mouth and let out blinding white light that temporally blinded the others.

"See you, sucker!" Euricus yelled and loomed into the cave.

"That's gotta be against the rules, " Ryan complained to Knur.

Knur shook his head. "This is on obstacle course. Nothing is against the rules."

"Seriously?" Ryan said. "Even eating the others?" Knur nodded grimly.

"I think I am beginning to understand why you don't want to compete in the game," Ryan said.

Suddenly, an arrow came piercing though the air. "Duck!" Ryan shouted. Knur dove down, narrowly missing it. A second later, a huge club swung down, sliding the dragon beside them in half.

"He'll get treated, right?" asked Ryan.

"Yeah. The Medical Dragons are especially trained for this," Knur replied.

"Phew. God to hear that," said Ryan.

"But if your wound is too serious, like this acid fog can do to you, " Knur nodded toward the yellowish gas slowly clouding up in front of them, "the Med dragons will just give you a shot of mountain troll blood, then you can die painlessly, " said Knur.

"The fog is blocking our only route! What are we going to do?" Ryan asked.

"There is a way. Using a protection spell that works like a shield"

"But how are we going to get one? I don't know any magic!

Knur smiled, "Watch and you'll see, " then, he opened his mouth and shouted, "HA!" A mint-green transparent plastic-like substance surrounded them both. "This works almost as well as the spell," Knur said proudly.

"What's that?" Ryan looked dumbfounded at the shield. He reached out to touch it, but the shield emitted a bunch of sparks that made Ryan cringe and pull his hand back.

"Careful, sending up sparks could cause it to break," Knur warned. "Each dragon has two to three different breath modes, and I found out I could exhale out a protective shield."

"Cool! And you said you suck at everything," said Ryan.

"But my power isn't as flashy as the other dragons. Look at Euricus then, his breathe mode is just so much better than mine. Even Booge, who is like the least popular dragon here except for me, has this really cool mode that can create a huge blizzard," said Knur.

"Those are for offense; you're made is for defense. They are completely different," Ryan said with a huff.

"Don't. You're only trying to cheer me up. That won't change anything. I'm accustomed to being alone. Euricus made sure that I'll never have any friends."

"Why does Euricus hate you so much?"

"Well... Keelia and I grew up together. And since he likes her so much..."

"So he's mean to you because he's jealous," Ryan confirmed.

"I... guess you could say that. Anyway, don't feel bad for me remember? I'm the dragon no one likes. The pathetic lonely dragon. Ending this game with both of us alive would be quite a miracle, so we'd better focus on the course now," Knur said as he swerved to avoid a mob of vicious bats with pointy fangs.

Suddenly Ryan screamed, "WATCH OUT!" A bright yellow dragon with blue markings slammed into them, causing Knur to almost fall down.

"Bad dragon!" Ryan shouted as if scolding a dog.

"Ryan, it's okay. Technically, this isn't against the rules, so don't get too mad. Rene's a playful dragon. He couldn't have possibly tried to hurt us on purpose."

"Then what about that?" said Ryan, pointing behind them. Two identical ocean blue dragons with dark red eyes were fighting, forming huge whirlwinds.

"That's Kelp and Yelp. They're twins, and they fight all the time," answered Knur. Just as he finished the sentence, the twins fell off the mountain they were fighting on.

Ryan laughed and Knur shot him a confused look. "It's not funny. Kelp and Yelp are two of the few dragons who are actually nice to me."

"No, I'm not laughing at them. It's just... Kelp and Yelp fell off the alp and yelled for help. Get it?" said Ryan, laughing so hard is almost fell off Knur's back.

Knur turned around to face Ryan and stared at him blankly.

"Never mind," Ryan said. Then he saw a golden flash that zigzagged into the right tunnel in front of them.

"Follow it, quick!" shouted Ryan. "The crown went into the right tunnel!"

Knur took Ryan and zoomed into the right tunnel. The crown was hovering in midair, as if waiting for their approach. "Faster!" Ryan urged Knur, and Knur picked up speed. Just when Ryan could reach out and grab it, the crown turned invisible. A second later, Euricus appeared in front of them, wearing the crown on his head and a big smirk on his face. "Thanks for the present! Like I said, you two are SO going to lose."

"That must be his annoying invisibility breath mode!" Knur exclaimed. "When we were younger, he used to turn invisible and push us into puddles of mud."

"Well, he certainly isn't going to get away with this," Ryan said through clenched teeth.

"What can you do anyway?" Euricus taunted.

"Yeah, Ryan. Just give up," Knur said sadly. "It'd be a miracle if we can even see him."

"See, the little guy knows when to stop. What about you?" said Euricus, smirking.

Ryan began to think. They couldn't see Euricus because technically, he was transparent like he's made of glass. But if Ryan could get some color on him...

Ryan pulled out a Color Splash and lobbed it at Euricus. A blob of hot pink landed on Euricus's back.

"Ew! I HATE pink! You're gonna pay for this, punk!" Euricus yelled.

"Well, you're gonna got some more, since you asked for it," answered Ryan.

"What did you throw at me? It smells like the time Knur ate too many stink radishes and had a nasty stomachache the next day."

"Um... If I remember correctly, that was you, Euricus," Knur said tentatively.

"Well, this is called a Color Splash. Perfect for showing stinky dragons who's the boss," Ryan said, letting another Color Splash fly at the same time. This time, a glob of bright orange landed on Euricus's belly, giving off a stench vaguely the rotten onions, burnt paper and leftovers mixed together with mud. Euricus started to scrape the goop off, but the more he tried, the messier he get. Finally, he had to let go of the crown in other to clean himself. Taking the chance, Knur and Ryan zoomed in, and Ryan grabbed the crown at the last second.

"Bye-bye, loser, " Ryan said as they flew out the exit.

"Be we really going to do this?" Ivy asked Travix, her violet eyes widening with worry.

"Cynthiana just told us specifically to harm Evelynda," said Travix.

"But..." Ivy began to say.

"We don't have any choice. Cynthiana has our life stones," Travix interrupted, staring at Ivy with the same violet eyes.

"I hate that stone," muttered Ivy.

"It's not our fault, Ivy, it's the curse."

"Can we really save our tribe by doing this, Travix? Or we be just lying to ourselves? It's just so confusing."

"Listen. All I know is that Cynthiana's got our stones, and we can find our tribe by it and hopefully undo the curse with my magic."

"Okay... But why Evelynda?"

"I don't know, Ivy! So shut up mouth and come help me make a plain!"

"Don't yell at me!" Ivy burst into tears.

"Ivy! Travix! Ryan's almost to the finish line! Where are you guys?" It was Lucas voice.

"Wipe your tears, sister. We've got work to do."

"Get outta the way, human. The crown's mine!" Euricus snarled, almost reaching them.

"You smell terrible, even worse than my egg salad sandwich I left in my locker for a whole semester," said Ryan, holding his nose.

Knur was small, but quick. However, Euricus was almost twice as big as Knur, and he moved with astonishing speed. He was catching up to the two of them, until Ryan reached into his bag, took out the dark blue jar of water nymph melodies, and opened it. Jessica had warned him to only use the jars as a last resort, and to him, the situation seemed just right.

The instant Ryan opened the jar, a high pitched note with several shrieks blasted out. A moment later, they mixed together into a black gaseous ball that headed straight for Euricus.

"That's all? A silly ball of air?" Euricus taunted. However, wherever the ball touched him, he withered in pain.

"That's probably kind of poison," said Ryan, "even though it's mostly attacking him, the ball must be giving off some toxic fumes. You better use that shield thingy again."

Knur obliged, and without Euricus bothering them, they flew to the finish line, Ryan proudly holding the crown high above his head.

Chapter 5

"Ryan, you did it!" Jessica ran over to Ryan and hugged him tightly.

"Good job, boy," Evelynda and Lucas both patted him on the back, even though Lucas made sure to be the first.

Travix and Ivy rushed forward and each gave him a high five.

"I told you the Color Splash would be useful," Ryan said proudly.

"I never knew Euricus looked so hot in pink," Knur said, obviously enjoying the moment. "Winning is a very nice thing, isn't it?"

"Attention!" said King Razi as he flew towards to the group. "The boy has proved himself worthy. I will now speak the location you are seeking: Acrakk."

"A crack? What kind of name is that?" said Jessica.

"Volcano Acrakk. A-C-R-A-K-K. It has been inactive for the past fifty years. The volcano can be divided into four parts: the Land of Red, the Lake of Darkness, the Tunnel of Ice, and the Chamber of Fire," said Lucas.

"There's a chamber inside a volcano? And what's up with ice?" asked Ryan.

"Well, you see, there are two old hags that live there. They're the owners of the volcano. The volcano itself reflects the mood they're in. One of them has a really, really bad temper; the other one is harsh and cold-blooded. So although there are many rare magical creatures there, no one dares to enter their territory and capture the creatures," said Evelynda. "Yes! I got to explain about the hags!"

"The key is inside the Chamber of Fire. There are thousands of keys floating on top of the lava. You'll need the box with you, but I don't know any thing else," said King Razi.

Euricus came bursting out of the tunnel, goop all over his body, "You want hot, I'll show you hot! " he said, then let out a huge blast of fire toward Ryan.

"Ryan!" Evelynda screamed. Lucas hurled himself in front of Ryan, getting a blast of fire in his face. Ryan, however, was unharmed. Everyone looked astounded.

"Why aren't you hurt?" Travix asked, blinking as if he couldn't believe his eyes.

"Yeah. Why?" Euricus echoed, astonished that a person could live through his most powerful blast of fire.

"I don't know either," Ryan was looking at his body unbelievably.

Jessica looked at Ryan suspiciously. "Did you, by any chance, happen to get inside the big box in the photo hanging on Cee's office?"

"You mean the huge microwave? Yeah," Ryan said slowly, not knowing where this was leading to.

"Then you've become fireproof," Jessica said, "I don't know how it happens, but Cee told me about the photo's abilities when I asked about it. I never believed it enough to try it myself, however, but now you've proved that it really works."

"Wow!" Ryan started to say, but they were interrupted by Ivy's yell, "HELP! Lucas is in big trouble. He needs help NOW!" Everyone turned to look at Lucas. His eyebrows and beard were both singed, and his face was badly scarred.

"Get him to the infirmary, now!" Evelynda barked. Everyone was surprised to see the usually nice and grandmotherly woman look and sound so worried.

"I... I'm sorry! Honestly! I was just so furious that I lost control and..." Euricus sputtered. Meanwhile, Knur carried Lucas away.

"...I mean, I'm really not a bad dragon! I love cuddly teddy bears and have a whole shelf of stuffed rainbow unicorns!" Euricus continued to say.

"Would you listen to that?" Knur came back right in time to hear the whole stuffed unicorn part.

"Yeah. Turns out that Euricus isn't as bad as we thought," said Ryan, doing a very bad job keeping a straight face.

"I'm a tree hugger, an animal lover, I'm Mother's favorite son!" Euricus wailed.

"Mama's boy!" exclaimed Ryan. Jessica, Travix, Ivy, and Knur burst out laughing and a bewildered Euricus turned to them.

"Did I... did I say that out loud?" he asked, embarrassed.

"You sure did," said Knur, barely containing his laughter.

"Maybe... we shouldn't take Lucas with us on our journey," said Jessica, looking worried.

"That old man will be just fine, except for the scars on his face. When I carried him to the infirmary, I also gave him a dose of my healing breath. He'll be fine in about ten minutes."

"You're got healing powers? That's awesome!" Ryan exclaimed.

"Yeah, you're the smallest, weakest, and the most useless of all dragons, " Euricus ignored Ryan and kept on saying, "but you always get the best of everything. Keelia talks about you all the time, you have the sweetest breath modes, and most people like you the second they lay their eyes on you. Everyone likes you but not me. That's not fair!"

"A lot of dragons like you too. You're got heaps of friends," reminded Knur.

"It's mostly because I'm stronger than them. They don't want to get on my bad side. Everyone's afraid of me," said Euricus, laughing sadly at himself.

"You're not as bad as you think you are. You just need smile more, laugh more, and most importantly, stop challenging others to a duel."

"But duels are the only time somebody actually cheers for me. I love it."

"Have you ever thought about how the opponent feels? No one likes to lose. Of course, duels are highly popular, and it is fun to watch one or two a week, but is it really necessary to ram the opponent's head into a wall every time you win?"

Euricus lowered his head, "Thank you, Knur. I know I've always been harsh on you but... would you be my friend?"

Knur looked shocked, but he managed to nod. "Yeah, of course."

"One last thing," said Euricus, "Don't tell anyone about the cuddly teddy bear incident." Then he flew away.

There was a commotion behind them. Everyone turned to see Lucas stumbling into the cavern.

"What are we still staying in this cave for? The king has already told us the location of the key. Let's go!"

"Um, don't you know what just happened? You just got hit by a blast of fire." Ryan said.

"Really? Well, that explains the scars on my face." Lucas touched the scars and laughed. "Anyway, let's get going!"

"Did the fire affect his mind?" Jessica whispered to Knur.

"Not only does that breath mode heal, it also erases all signs of the incident, so the people won't be too traumatic about it. Play along for a few hours."

"Why is the annoying fortune teller still in their group?" Cynthiana said as she impatiently crossed her legs.

"Maybe they didn't hear their orders correctly," said the man in black.

"Children's are useless and ungrateful," Cynthiana announced. "How old are they? Eleven, twelve ..."

"They are both fourteen," the man interrupted, earning a cold glare from Cynthiana.

"As I was saying, that Travix boy is way too hateful. And the girl," she shuddered, "the girl never obeys any rules. She's even worse than the boy."

"They will follow their order, love. I'll make sure to send them another message," he said. Then he bowed and walked out the room.

"So, I guess it's finally time to say goodbye," Ryan said to Knur.

"Yeah. Hope you'll fulfill your quest," said Knur.

"Why don't you come with us then? It'll be fun to have you with us," Travix chimed in.

Knur shook his head. "I need to stay to help Euricus. He's right. A lot of dragons are afraid of him. I'll try my best to help him."

"You'll do a great job. I know it," Jessica said, smiling gently.

"Now that you know your destination, you better get going," Knur said as he stepped backwards and gave Ryan a said smile. With one final wave, the little dragon flew away and disappeared in the clouds.

"Anyone got some Dustrix?" Jessica asked.

Seeing Ryan's confused look, Ivy answered before he could ask, "Dustrix be a magic, sparkly powder that we need to use when we be making a portal."

Evelynda reached in to her cloak and pulled out a small container. She uncorked it and sprinkled pale gold dust in a circle. "Good thing I just got a refill at the Grand Taske Market."

Seconds later, a swirl of bright purple materialized. It stretched to the size of a regular door.

Taking a deep breath, Ryan stepped into the portal first.

The moment Ryan passed through the portal, his first thought was: Wow, it's really hot. The others came through the portal, and after a few minutes, all of their faces were beaded with sweat.

"Whoa, that's one big volcano," Lucas said, gazing up at the peak. It loomed over them, the bright red lava shimmering in the glare of the noonday sun. The ground they were standing on was covered with chunks of the red lava. However, since the sun was so hot, it felt as if they were standing in a red lava desert.

"And that," Evelynda gestured behind her, "is the Land of Red." Jessica bent down to touch the sand. When she pulled it up, her hand was covered in red dust. "Really red," she muttered.

"We should probably eat the Fruity Mixers, since the hags remember every intruder that goes into the volcano, so we can't let them know our real identities. We don't know exactly how long the Fruity Mixers will last, so if we want to get the key by sundown, we'd better take them now," Lucas said.

Jessica held out the sack of the colorful fruit, and everyone took one.

"These look really weird," Ryan commented, turning his rounding his hand. It looked like a bright blue peach with green stripes. He took a big bite, and it tasted like lemonade, sweet and sour, but with a hint of mint in it too. Also, the fruit had a fizzy taste that started slowly, gradually becoming more intense, and started to spread all over his body. Ryan felt the tingling sensation increase to its extreme point, eventually slowing down and finally stopping.

"Wow, you look like you're from Romania!" Jessica said, and seeing Ryan's blank look, she hastily added, "You know, where vampires are." Ryan looked down at his hands. They were really pale and when Ivy held out a mirror to him, he saw that he now had black hair, dark eyes and sharp features.

"Well, you're a redhead!" said Ryan as he handed Jessica the mirror.

"Gah! My hair!" screamed Jessica. Her long black hair was now bright red and only fell to her shoulders. "I'm all freckly," she complained.

"I believe we're now Chinese," said Travix.

"We still look like twins," said Ivy. Both of their hair was straight and jet black and they had an Asian skin tone. Only their eyes remained the same, violet with a silver iris.

"Interesting..." said Lucas. At first the others couldn't even recognize him. The old man was African now, with chocolatety black skin and short curly gray hair.

"Hah! You look like a piece of charcoal, old man!" laughed Evelynda.

"Um, you might want to take a look at yourself," said Ryan. Evelynda looked at the mirror and shrieked. Her face was covered with warts and scars. Her nose was crooked with a large bump on it. Plus, her skin was a sickly green.

"I'm green! Ahhhhhh!" Evelynda went hysterical. She zoomed around them, waving her hands up in the air as she screamed.

"Watch out!" Travix yelled suddenly. As soon as his words left his mouth, Evelynda tripped on a piece of hardened lava, fell into the hole in front of her, and disappeared.

The land rumbled, causing a fierce sandstorm. When the wind died, they noticed that the hole itself disappeared.

"That sinkhole that took Evelynda, well, it got rid of her for us," Travix said to Ivy. "Now I won't have to face my guilty conscience anymore."

"Travix?" Ivy asked, "Will Cynthiana be mad that we didn't harm Evelynda personally?"

"Who cares that much? She told us to harm Evelynda. Evelynda fell into a sinkhole. Falling into a sinkhole equals being harmed. Can't you understand the simplest math?"

"That not be math! It be different and you know it! I be telling Jessica the others about Cynthiana, since you be no help."

"You dare?"

"YES!"

Jessica was surprised when Ivy came to her, a big pleading look in her eyes. "Jessica, will you mad if I tell you something?" she asked.

"Depends on what you say," Jessica answered.

"Travix and I....," Ivy started to say, but Travix butted in and said, "What she means is, that we think you actually are pretty good-looking for a red head."

"Okay...." Jessica had a confused look on her face. Using the chance, Travix pulled Ivy away.

Ryan was daydreaming about ice cream sundaes when Jessica came over to him.

"I think Ivy wants to tell us a secret that Travix is determined to keep."

"No... I want a double fudge ice cream, not strawberry..." said Ryan absentmindedly.

"Snap out of it," Jessica commanded. "And my water bottle is not an ice cream cone!"

"Wha – What?"

"I said, Ivy and Travix are keeping a secret!"

"So? A lotta people have secrets. What's the big deal?"

"Don't you think they act really weird sometimes?"

Ryan did a facepalm. "Don't tell me you're still suspicious about them."

"If you don't believe me, then I'm going to investigate myself!" Jessica stormed away.

"Ryan, can I talk to you?" asked a timid voice. It was Ivy.

"Sure," Ryan replied.

"I, um, I overheard Jessica and you talking and..."

"I don't believe her. You guys are weird, that's true, but nice," he interrupted.

"That be what I want to tell you about. Travix and I be the last survives among our tribe. Because of our vivid violet eye color, a lot of merchants hire hunters to get our eyes. Cynthiana murdered our family and friends then adopted us. Of course we fought back at first, but in some way, she got our life stones. That be another trait of our tribe. Whatever happens to our life stones will happen to us. For example, if you burn it, we will feel fire on us. We won't really catch on fire, but we will feel the same pain. So we ended up as apprentices of Cynthiana. She made us do a lot of horrible things, and now she wants us to harm you guys. I don't know what to do!" Ivy broke into sobs and collapsed on the ground.

Ryan froze, and then said with a strained smile, "You're not feeling very well. It must be the heat. Get some rest." He bent down to lift her up.

"No. It's true." Travix said as he emerged from a large red rock. "We are assigned to report back to Cynthiana whenever you've made a move. We were previously assigned to harm Evelynda but the sinkhole did it before us. Our meeting was never by accident. Come, Ivy, I don't think we are wanted here anymore." His voice was as hard as steel and as cold as ice. When he walked over to help Ivy up, Ryan noticed that he was visibly shaking.

"Hey," Ryan said softly. "I don't care if you're a spy or not. Even if you intended to harm us, you never did. So in my point of view, you're still my friend, a part of my group, and the same helpless boy who was stuck on the tree with his sister."

"See, Travix, I knew Ryan would understand!" said Ivy, smiling brightly at her brother.

Travix winced, "I guess... Thank you, Ryan."

"It's about time you confessed," said Lucas coming out from behind a rock, followed by Jessica. Jessica shot Ryan an "I told you so" look and this time, Ryan winced.

"From the second I met you I recognized Cynthiana's magic in you," Lucas clarified.

"Yeah, I always thought there was something eerie about the way you two always huddled together taking among yourselves," Jessica chimed in.

"We don't want to follow Cynthiana's orders, but if we don't, she always thinks of terrible punishments for us. She also has a loyal assistant. Whoever he is we don't know, but he's always dressed in black from head to toe. They have ways of knowing our every move, so we're probably in tremendous trouble by telling you this," Travix said.

"Hey, we're a team now. If some of us are in trouble, the rest will surely rush to their aid. We'll find a way to work this out, if we're all willing to help. All for one and one for all, right?" Jessica said.

"Yeah!" Ryan, Travix, Ivy, and Lucas shouted together.

"Now we need to devise a plan," Lucas said. They had walked for an hour or so, and were approaching the Lake of Darkness.

"We need a plan that can take us to the center of the volcano and get the key, while another plan can help us defeat Cynthiana." Travix said.

"Why don't we split up into two groups?" Ivy suggested. "That way, we can accomplish more things at the same time."

"That's a good idea," Lucas agreed. "Ryan and Jessica go into the volcano, while the twins and I go attack Cynthiana."

"Are you sure? Ryan and aren't experienced..." Jessica's voice trailed off. As much as she wanted to prove herself, she was still nervous about going into the volcano without a skilled person.

"You two are the perfect team. Ryan's skilled with his sword and you're pretty good at magic. Don't worry, you'll be fine." Lucas assured them.

"So it's all set," Travix said.

"Call us when you're in trouble, and we'll go there as fast as we can," Ivy added.

"You too, " Jessica said.

"We'll go to the E.Y.E. headquarters first," Lucas commanded.

"Lucky I got the dust thingy from Evelynda before," Ryan said, handing Travix the vial. Travix muttered his thanks as he concentrated.

A portal popped out and Lucas turned to Ryan, "One last thing, find Evelynda for me, will you?" Then they walked in and the portal disappeared.

Now, only Ryan and Jessica were left. They were standing beside a huge lake with only a sword and a magic wand to protect them. Lucas and the twins had taken the bag of Color Splashes with them, but Ryan and Jessica kept the Fruity Mixers, in case theirs wore off. They also got two jars of the melodies, the purple one and the brown one.

"How can we get past this lake?" Ryan asked as he tossed a rock to the middle of it. A huge figure jumped out, gobbled the rock, and splashed back into the murky water.

"Holy moly! Look at the size of its teeth! I'm not swimming across it!" Ryan yelped, scrambling away from the lake.

Jessica stared thoughtfully at the lake, and then flashed a devilish smile at Ryan." I think I know what to do."

"You sure this is the E.Y.E. headquarters?" Lucas asked, eyeing suspiciously at the empty hallway. "It seems to be awfully quiet."

"It really be," said Ivy, "Right, Travix?"

Travix was silent for a while, and then he said, "I've been thinking. Don't you think we're passed this hallway before?" He traced the intricate carvings on the wall with one finger. "See this little dent? I saw one exactly the same half an hour ago."

"But that be impossible! We've been here for hours now and there be only one path!" said Ivy.

"Unless," Travix smiled, "this hallway is shaped like a –"

"Circle! You're a genius, boy!" exclaimed Lucas.

"Cynthiana's toying with us," Travix confirmed. "She knows that we're here."

"Well said, young man," a cheerful voice said. "A pity that we have to kill you now. You'll make such a powerful warlock." A man wearing a long white robe stepped through a portal that suddenly appeared in front of them.

"Behave yourself, Seppkumis. The mistress told us only to hold them as captives," growled a low voice. Another man wearing a dark gray cloak walked out, his face entirely covered by the hood.

"Awww, Xan, you're no fun!" the man in white robes, Seppkumis, pouted.

"Orders are orders, you know we can't disobey Mistress Cynthiana," Xan answered.

"Hold on, who are you guys?" Travix asked.

"We are your replacements!" Seppkumis answered gleefully. "After you little traitors betrayed Mistress Cynthiana, she hired us to work in your places."

"We be no traitors! We only stand up for ourselves!" Ivy was so mad that she has already loaded up her bow, Goldenflight, and was pointing the arrow straight at Seppkumis's heart.

"Calm down, Ivy." Lucas soothed her. "What do you want?" he asked them.

"To keep you foul, backstabbing, worthless traitors away from Mistress Cynthiana's plans of course!"

"THAT'S IT! I've had enough!" Ivy bellowed. For such a pretty little girl, she could be quite loud if she wanted to. At the same time, she let her arrow fly. It should have landed on Seppkumis's heart, but he deflected it with an ivory shield. In his other hand, he held a long spear. Xan, on the other hand, reached into his robes and took out a platinum wand.

"What's your magic level?" Lucas asked.

"Clear diamond and going up, while you, are going down." Xan answered. Then he shouted, "ATTACK!" A herd of galloping desks raced out from every corridor and stamped toward them. Lucas raised his hand, and then all of the wooden desks fell apart into sticks that were beating Xan on his head.

The same time, Ivy and Travix were taking on Seppkumis. Ivy shot arrow after arrow, some tipped with rusty blades, while others carried nets that entangled Seppkumis. However, with his spear, those didn't stop him for long.

"You're dead, girl, " he growled, and was about to stab Ivy, when a gust of wind picked him up and set him ten feet away. He turned around to see Travix glaring at him.

"No one touches my little sister," he said, then waved his wand. "BURN!" Seppkumis looked down and saw his white robe catching fire.

51

"Ahhh! Omigod! Omigod! Help!" he screamed like a little girl, frantically running around.

"You two are pathetic," said a childish voice. No one had noticed the portal until a little girl stepped out. Her strawberry blond hair was pulled back into pigtails and she looked no more than seven years old. Yet her sinister coal black eyes made her seem much older. She snapped her fingers, then the fire on Seppkumis extinguished and the sticks that were previously attacking Xan fell down on the floor in a pile.

"Thanks, Nausicaa!" said Seppkumis. Xan grunted a thank you and Nausicaa rolled her eyes.

"Seriously, I can't believe an idiot like you really is a clear diamond... Oh! By the way, my name is Nausicaa. Level clear diamond like him too, hence this magnificent brain," she said.

"Just how many apprentices does Cynthiana have?" asked Travix, annoyed.

"I'm not an apprentice. We're just hire to capture you," she replied, looking slightly offended, "I'm must say that I miscalculated your ability. Apparently these two aren't capable, so I came." She shrugged. "Okay. Back to work. Seppkumis, take the girl. Xan, the boy. And I, will get the old man." She lifted her right hand, revealing a gleaming silver ring with sparking diamond encrusted on the middle, and snapped her finger.

Shimmering walls of magic divided the wide hallway into three parts. Seppkumis and Ivy in one part, Xan and Travix in another, leaving Nausicaa ad Lucas in the remaining part.

"Ivy!" Travix cried, and ran towards her. But the instant he hit the wall, a tremendous shot of electricity sent him flying through the air.

"Oh no you don't," scolded Nausicaa, shaking a finger accusingly at Travix. "Everyone fights their own fight."

"Oh, and, new orders that even I approve from that homicidal maniac, " she smiled, looking completely innocent; "we fight to the death."

Chapter 6

"Don't look down, don't look down, don't look down..." Ryan kept chanting to himself. Jessica had enchanted a boulder beside the lake and made it hover in the air. Jessica was now standing on top of it and steering them, while Ryan was underneath the boulder, grabbing on to any handholds he could find.

The precise reason why he was dangling perilously under the boulder was because Jessica told him to. When he tried to argue, she gave him all sorts of reasons that made him finally give in. "You'll need to distract the monster so I can concentrate on steering. The rock can't handle both of our weight. You'll actually be safer down there."

"Just a few more yards!" Jessica yelled down to him, but he wasn't listening. A second ago the monster had lifted its head out of the water and sniffed. Ryan couldn't speak because he was sure that the monster had caught their scent. And the sight of the monster's head, with its yellow eyes, rows of teeth, and huge nostrils, made Ryan shudder with fear, almost losing his grip on the boulder.

Ryan scanned the water. The surface was smooth as a mirror without a sign of the fish-like monster. He felt a drop of sweat, slowly dripping down his forehead. "No! No! No!" He thought, and tried desperately to wipe it off with his sleeve. Realizing that it wasn't going to work, he lifted his head high up, trying to force the bead of sweat back. But it still stubbornly dripped down, fell toward the lake, and broke the mirror-like surface.

This instant it hit the surface, the monster jumped out, eyes shining greedily with a look at Ryan that clearly meant "lunch".

"Faster, Jessica! Faster!" Ryan screamed, clinging on the boulder with all his might.

The monster jumped again, this time almost reaching Ryan's right foot. "Quick! Go higher!"

"I'm trying! Shut up!" yelled Jessica, rapidly increasing the height. However, the boulder was staring to wobble.

"What's wrong?" Ryan shouted.

"I'm pushing the rock too hard. It can't handle that much magic!" Jessica said frantically.

"Then don't force it so!"

"You want to be eaten by that monster?"

Ryan stopped cold. He definitely didn't want to be eaten, but to choose between the monster jumping up and eating him part by part, or being tossed into theater and eaten whole, he would much rather choose the latter and held on tight. Real tight.

"I think I've got it!" Jessica shouted.

"What?"

"Jump."

"WHAAAT?!"

"Jump! I promise I'll catch you. Listen, we're well above the water, but the rock can't handle us anymore. The same time you jump, throw a Fruity Mixer to the other side of the lake. Hopefully, the monster will be distracted and go after it instead of you."

"Hopefully?"

"It's the only chance we have. Are you doing it of not?"

Ryan closed his eyes. "Here we go," and dropped. At the same time, he took out a Fruity Mixer and threw it as far as he could, hoping for the best.

To his amazement, the plan really worked. The Fruity Mixer in a grotesque color of rotten bananas flying through the air caught the monster's attention instead of Ryan freefalling into the dark, cold water. With a single gigantic gulp, the monster swallowed the Fruity Mixer whole then disappeared into the depths of the lake. Jessica took the chance to snatch Ryan out of the water and safely onto the shore.

"Thanks," he muttered, "why couldn't you just conjure something to get us safely across instead of that awful rock?"

Jessica huffed, "it's impossible to conjure objects out of nowhere. We can bewitch and summon objects, but we can never make things appear out of thin air. Hey, you're all wet." With a wave of her wand, Ryan's clothes magically became dry in an instant.

Ryan rubbed his hands together. "So, what next?"

"The Tunnel of Ice," Jessica replied as she pointed forward. The sun was setting, casting an orange yellow glow on everything. But the looming mountain before them was completely black and covered with a thin layer of mist. A cave glowing with faint blue light was barely visible because of it.

"It sure looks... creepy, " said Ryan.

"Come on!" Jessica pulled Ryan and they headed to the mountain.

Travix sucked in his breath as fire snaked around his right arm. With a flick of his wand he sent a bolt of lighting forward Xan, who easily dodged it.

"You're good, but still not my level," said Xan, smirking.

"Shut it." Travix said coldly. He tried to concentrate on magic, but he always found himself worrying about how Ivy was doing. His sister was his only family left in the world, and he would do anything to protect her.

"Seppkumis is pretty good with his spear, boy. I doubt the girl will make it. Hmmm... What should we make do of her once we've captured her? Such a pretty little girl, isn't she? Oh, wait. Nausicaa said we had to right until one of us dies. What a loss," Xan sighed and wiped an imaginary tear.

Travix's blood boiled. His sister would make it. She had to. He blasted another bolt of lightning that was so fierce that it paralyzed Xan and Xan collapsed on the floor. Travix walked towards him and raised his wand, preparing to strike. However, his wand felt oddly heavy in his hand, and Travix couldn't bring himself to kill Xan, despite how evil or dangerous he was.

"Nausicaa! I want a word!" Travix called. She stopped fighting Lucas and walked through the shimmering wall as if it wasn't there.

"Oh wow!" She exclaimed, pretending to be shocked. "You defeated a person with a higher level of magic than you! I'm so scared!" She said with a mocking voice.

"Cut the theatrics. Let's talk deals. You let us go unharmed, and I won't kill Xan. If you don't, well, you know what would happen."

"Oh, but killing is part of this game! You're so nice, kind, and pathetic," she said, her black eyes boring into Travix's. "Can't bring you to finish him off, huh? Well, I'll just take over your job and finish you at the same time, then." Nausicaa raised her hand. Threads of fiery red burst from the tip of her ring and coiled around Xan, becoming tighter, and eventually strangling him. After what seemed like hours, but actually was a few minutes, Nausicaa waved her hand again. The threads released Xan, and the would-be great person was no more.

"Behold, the Tunnel of Ice!" Ryan said in an exaggerated dramatic voice.

"Quiet, now. There might be something lurking inside the cave, waiting for us in ambush."

"I know, that's why I'm being silly. If we were both as serious as you, that something lurking inside would be jubilant to see us, 'cause it would want to get rid of all the tension and eat us. If at least one of us is smiling, it would think that we aren't scared of it. Other than that, we're going into a tunnel made of ICE! Isn't it cool?"

"If you say so, but it is never wrong to stay cautious, and— oh my god, what is that?"

The interior of the tunnel was, well, untunnel-like with bright ice crystals hovering above their heads giving off pale blue light and clear ice pillars around them reflecting the lights. Suspended with magic in front of them were a line of floating obstacles made of ice as well.

There were three blocks of ice floating knee-high in front of them. The blocks were moving left and right parallel to the platform they were standing on, yet in opposite directions. Behind the ice blocks was a large seesaw moving up and down. Even further behind was a single windmill with four blades turning clockwise. They could see a small golden light at the end of the tunnel, inviting them with its warm glow.

Jessica peered down the edge of the platform. "It's impossible to go down there. We're way up." She squinted then continued, "I can see some ice caps. Part of the water might even be frozen. The only way across would be through the obstacles."

Ryan studied the block of ice in front of him, waited for the right moment, and then jumped. He landed in the center of the block, almost losing his balance. "Kinda slippery," he said, "Otherwise this isn't too hard. Come on, Jess!" Gathering his concentration, he leaped again. He could hear Jessica following him from behind. The final jump was the trickiest, for the blocks of ice were lined up by size, the last being the smallest. Finally, he arrived at a platform just enough for his two feet to stand on. Waiting in front was the giant seesaw.

With a quick jump, he landed in the middle. The seesaw kept bumping up and down, like two invisible children were playing on it. Tentatively he took a step forward, and was immediately lifted up into the air then down on his back with a bang.

"Ryan!" Jessica screamed, sprinting to the platform in front of the seesaw, watching him worriedly.

"I'm okay. We have to use its force to lead us safely across. Don't stay still, or you'll end up like I just did. My mates and I often do this kind of stuff. Trust me." Back at home, Ryan and his friends often set up makeshift obstacle courses in the park, including wobbling over a teetering seesaw. This was basically the same, only that the stakes were higher and it was a lot more slippery and challenging.

Behind the seesaw was a balance beam about a foot wide. The windmill's blades were blocking the path in the middle as they rotated, designed to send people cascading down to the icy depths. Ryan walked slowly across, spreading his arms out to keep his balance. When he got to the middle, he looked at the blades, trying to figure out the time pattern when the blades came in contact with the path. After a moment, he got down on his stomach and carefully made his way across when the exit came into view.

"The blades of the icy windmill thingy never really touch the path. The key is to get down low and never lift your head. If you try to pass it standing up, you'll be knocked down in no time," Ryan called back to Jessica. However, instead of a reply, he was answered by a piercing scream that echoed all over the glistening tunnel.

"Jessica!" Ryan shouted. Frantically turning around, he saw Jessica still frozen at the platform leading to the revolving seesaw, trembling in fear. He started back, passing the giant windmill to the head of the balance beam. There he stopped and looked at Jessica.

"Ryan, help," Jessica looked at him, fear in her eyes. Even though it was just a plea, Ryan knew that he had to help get her safely across. He didn't need a reason, he just knew.

"Listen. Focus on what I say. This isn't really has hard as it seems. I know it looks all high up and scary," Jessica glanced down, and let out a small squeak.

"Don't. Just look at me. You're gonna be fine. Step forward, and jump when I tell you to, okay?" She managed to nod, slowly inching forwards. Eyes trained on the seesaw, Ryan shouted, "Jump!"

She did not. Jessica stood there, paralyzed, staring at the frozen water down below. A split second later, she was thrown into the air, a silent scream stuck in her opened mouth.

Almost instinctively, Ryan reached out, grasping her right arm firmly, pulling her to the balance beam. He winced as his back came in contact with the cold, hard ice, and even more so when he felt something bump into his nose. He could swear that he almost saw stars by the force of the impact. Grimacing, he cracked open one eye, only to find Jessica blushing like the setting sun. He briefly wondered if she was about to get a nosebleed judging the way she was cupping her nose and her bright crimson cheeks, then reached out to check.

Before he could touch her, Jessica let out a small shriek and scooted backward, only to be pulled back to him by his hand that was still clasped on her arm.

Her blush increased tenfold. She seemed to be scared, even terrified, for her eyes were cast downwards and she was biting her lower lip.

That was when he finally noticed that he had a princess sprawled on top of him. They scrambled away from each other once he loosened his grip on her arm, and Ryan could feel his own cheeks heating up.

They passed the remaining obstacle without any difficulty. Together, they walked towards the exit of the tunnel.

Ivy shot another arrow at Seppkumis. A sharp golden needle was hidden inside the tip, and would prick the opponent then cause a deep sleep. It was her final arrow, so she prayed, "Please let it work, please let it work." However, her prayers went unanswered. Seppkumis blocked it and leered at her, " Pretty little girl has no arrows now. What will she do?"

Ivy had a sudden burst of inspiration, but she was hesitant. She picked up the bag of Color Splashes and muttered, "I can't believe I be doing this." Then she chose a slimy, gruesome green one and threw it toward Seppkumis as hard as she could. He raised his shield, but the ball soared above it and smacked him right in the face.

"Gah! What did you threw on my face?" Seppkumis demanded. The blackish-green liquid was slowly bubbling and dripping to the floor. A strong odor of mold and socks that haven't been washed for a year filled the whole hallway.

"What's with the disgusting smell?" Nausicaa screeched. "I just finished washing my hair for two hours using Cherry Blossom Fragrance and the odor is ruining it! Uh, I'm in no mood of killing you now, boy. I'll just finish old man off and get outta here!"

"Hey! I'm stuck!" Seppkumis cried. His feet were stuck on the ground and his right hand was also stuck to his foot by trying to remove it. "What is this slop?"

"Color Splashes, at your service," Ivy chipped in. "Who knew, right?" She winked at her brother.

Travix smiled. It took a lot to defeat his sister. He glanced at Lucas. The old man was panting and half of his shirt was burned, but otherwise he was fine.

Nausicaa was fuming. That Lucas old man wasn't supposed to be here according to the information Cynthiana provided, and as if it wasn't enough, that old man was a level higher than her, making him even harder to kill.

"I'm utterly disappointed with you, Seppkumis. Oh well, those who are stronger are the only ones who can survive in this cruel world. I guess I have to do the dirty work again since that lovely little girl is most certainly not capable of doing it," Nausicaa sneered, and raised her hand.

"Wait! He be part of your team! How could you?" Ivy cried. She spread her arms out protectively in front of Seppkumis.

"He's useless, and people like him deserve to die," Nausicaa answered. "Don't be a fool; you've already won your battle."

"No one deserves to die! You be mean!" Ivy shouted.

Nausicaa ignored her and flicked her wrist. White hot flames burst out of her ring and shot forward Ivy.

Ivy's face was contorted with fury. "You dare kill me?" She shouted.

Nausicaa smiled wickedly, "Exactly what I'm doing." She raised he hand again, and the flames moved even faster.

"Ivy!" Travix shouted, but Nausicaa pointed her ring at him, forbidding him to go closer. Travix saw Ivy's face, wide-eyed and frightened, the flames getting closer each second.

"Um," Ryan said slowly, "What's next?"

Regaining her composure, Jessica led the way, saying briskly at the same time, "Either we find the key or we don't. The Chamber of Fire."

A few minutes of walking led them to another tunnel that was lit up with tons of shimmering floating lights. Ryan tried to catch one, but they zoomed away the moment he came close. Jessica clicked her tongue, and he hurried to catch up with her. Finally, they came to a door. On it was a plaque that read.

The chamber beholds the things you'll use
Utter the phrase, it won't refuse

'Revye eky dolhs eth lnoy hurtt'
May all the secrets be unraveled

"The third line is written in Polish! How can we understand what we're supposed to say? Are we just going to speak the weird sentence that way?" Ryan asked.

Jessica held up a finger. "That isn't Polish. As far as I know, it isn't any language we know. However, the rest is written in English, so I bet there is a way to figure it out."

"How?"

"The last sentence mentioned 'unravel'..." she paused and thought for a moment. Then she smiled. "Do you know what an anagram is?"

"An ana– what?"

"Hmm, I thought so. An anagram is a puzzle when the letters in a word or phrase are in the wrong order. Simply speaking, you need to unscramble the letters."

"So it's just a word puzzle."

"Correct. How about 'Reevy yek dolhs het lony thurt'? It sounds a little like gnomish mixed with a bit of old world fae language..." Jessica went on mumbling.

"Um, Jess? How about 'Every key holds the only truth'? It sounds a bit like plain English, right?" Ryan teased.

Jessica turned red. "It's not my fault that I always think more complicated!"

"Yeah, yeah. So you ready?" Ryan asked as he placed his hands on the heavy double doors.

"As I'll ever be," Jessica muttered. The same time, Ryan pushed open the doors.

Chapter 7

Glamorous.

It was the only word that could describe the chamber. The walls shone like moonlight. Jewels were embedded on the ceiling like twinkling stars. A black fountain rested at the center of the circular room, but instead of water, bluish-green fire danced in it, casting a mysterious glow around. However, the most impressive of all was all the keys that were floating around. Keys that were made of pure gold, keys that looked like what little girls used to lock their diaries, keys just like the ones people use to lock doors. Jail keys, skeleton keys, car keys, any keys a person could imagine.

Both of them stepped gently into the room, for fear of disturbing anything. Yet, within a few paces into the room, a blast of fire shot up from the ground just a couple feet from them. Ryan scanned the room. He could see burst of fire shooting up randomly from the floor like geysers everywhere.

Beside him, Jessica shrieked and leaped into Ryan's arms, trying to shield herself from the pillar of fire that just appeared beneath her feet. If she hadn't reacted so quickly, she would've caught the full force of the blast.

Quickly untangling herself from Ryan, Jessica said urgently, "I can't stay in here. I wouldn't last ten minutes if I did. You have your fireproof powers and now's the best time to put them to use. I'll wait in the corridor, okay?" Without waiting for a response, she stepped back into the hallway, watching Ryan carefully through the open doors.

"How am I going to solve the puzzle? It'll take us forever to figure out which key we need!" Ryan whined.

"Utter the phrase, it won't refuse..." Jessica was muttering to herself under her breath. She paced back and forth in deep thought. A few minutes later, she called to Ryan with a huge grin on her face.

"We just need to recite the sentence and the key will appear!"

"You sure?"

"It's possible, maybe even probable. The plaque said that 'Utter the phrase, it won't refuse', so the chamber will probably give us the key."

"Okay....." Ryan stood carefully in the center of the room beside the fountain. On the count of three, he said loudly, "Every key holds the only truth."

A rumbling from the fountain caught their attention. Another sign had risen from the floor. Ryan hurried over to see it and read it aloud to Jessica, who was hovering around the doorway in curiosity.

Keep on going now don't give up
You're ONE step away to finding your clue
Decipher the sentence down below,
The Key TO A journey will soon begin
S KW NYSXQ DRSC PYB DRO QBOKDOB QYYN

"Why are the letter Ks capitalized?" Ryan asked.

"One step away..." Jessica mumbled, pacing back and forth.

"Hey! What's that?" Ryan suddenly yelled. He was pointing at the other side of the fountain. A double-layered wheel labeled with alphabets rose from the ground. One wheel was larger than the other, and the letters were carved in other around the edges, so when Ryan spun the smaller wheel, its letters were always directly underneath the bigger wheel's letters.

"It's a wheel," Jessica said flatly.

"Thank you, genius," Ryan said, rolling his eyes.

"Wait, I know! K to A!" Jessica exclaimed.

"Huh?"

"Don't just stand there! Go spin the wheel!"

"What for?"

"Move the letter K on the small wheel underneath the letter A on the big wheel. Do it now!!"

After Ryan had moved the wheel, then Jessica exclaimed, "It's a code. K equals A, L equals B, M equals C, and so on. Now all we have to do is exchange the letters in the sentence for the ones they really stand for. Got a pen and piece of paper?"

Ryan dumped the contents of his backpack on the floor. Several half eaten chocolate bars and a sparkly pink pen fell out. He walked to the door and gave it to her.

Jessica raised her eyebrows. "You like pink. Seriously?"

"It's the best I could find in the pile of junk that Cee let me choose my supplies from."

"That'll do," Jessica said, "A piece of paper?" Ryan handed her a pink notebook with hearts on the cover. She shook her head, but didn't say anything. Jessica copied down the sentence then started writing down the correct letters, occasionally asking Ryan for help. A few minutes later, she angled the notebook for Ryan to see and they chorused, "I am doing this for the greater good."

A minute passed. Nothing happened. The keys continued to floating around them, but none came toward. Then out of the corner of his eye, Ryan saw his backpack shaking violently. The moment he unzipped it, the silver key chain Cee had given him shot out, a certain charm flashing brightly. It was a small silver key, nothing special, but it shone with such brilliance that Ryan knew instantly it was the one.

Golden words appeared in midair, and formed a sentence.

You sincerely meant the words you said; the key of truth is now rightfully yours.

"What the... So it's there all the time? Why would–" Ryan mumbled incoherently.

"The box! Here, open it!" Jessica said excitedly, unbeknown to the fact that the key was from Ryan's backpack, rather than all the other keys around them, for she had been busy searching around the chamber.

Ryan stuck the key in the small keyhole underneath the box, turned it a hundred and eighty degrees, and slowly pried it open.

Travix couldn't believe what just happened. For the past fourteen years, he had worked so hard keeping his little sister safe, but now he couldn't do anything but watch the deadly flames getting nearer and nearer her. He quietly reached into his pocket to get his wand, trying to seem motionless at the same time.

"Oh, don't bother," Nausicaa said, giggling. "But I will give you one more chance." She flicked her wrist, and the fire halted. Silver chains sprouted from the ground, imprisoning Ivy. "A deal. You join us, and I'll release both the girl and the old man." She pointed to the other side of the hallway, where Lucas was desperately trying to break the chains with magic. "You won't be able to harm it. It's magic-proof. Cost me five hundred zarae, but totally worth it," she addressed Lucas. "So," she swung her gaze back at Travix, "your answer?"

"Don't do it. Travix! I'll be fine, really!" Ivy yelled, tears brimming from her eyes. "I be serious! You do it and I will hate you forever!"

Travix glanced at Lucas. The old man pointed at Nausicaa's head. At first Travix didn't get it, but when Lucas mimed combing his hair, Travix knew what to do.

"This is my answer," he said to Nausicaa. He picked up a purple Color Splash, and with the briefest hesitation, threw it towards Nausicaa's hair. It burst all over her hair and face, turning her into a purple faced monster with two purple pigtails, screaming insults at everyone within a five mile radius.

"You awful, insulting, pathetic, idiotic, stupid, jerkish imbecile!" She screamed at Travix. He was just wondering how she managed to say that much in one breath, when Seppkumis ran out from behind Ivy and caught Nausicaa in a stranglehold. She screamed, begging him to let her go, but he gripped her throat even tighter. The fury in his face was more than evil. It was pure hatred. With a fierce roar and a quick snap, he took away Nausicaa's life.

Ryan couldn't fully express his emotion. Shock, anger, or disbelief? He glanced at Jessica, who was crouching on the floor with a sick expression on her face.

An eye was in the box. Jade green, with flecks of gold around the pupil. It was unmistakably Cynthiana's. Ryan wasn't sure what he should do with it.

"It's her eye," Jessica said, her voice barely above a whisper. "That's why she wears an eye patch, because she lost it."

"I don't get it. We've come this far just for her stupid eye? I do not understand, I really don't," Ryan muttered.

A piece of paper poked out from under the dark red piece of satin the eye was on. Ryan gingerly took it out, being carefully not to touch the eye, and unfolded it carefully. He drew in a breath as he started to read the contents of the paper.

When I was a young girl, I was used to being listened to. Everyone did what I told them to, even if it meant harm to them. A lot of people despised me, but even more admired and adored me. I had tons of loving fans who answered to my every command. No one ever dared to say "No" to me. I was the best. Until one particular incident happened. No matter how hard I try to forget, the memory is etched in my mind. I can't believe it's just an act. All of his loving smiles, caring words, and soothing embraces were pretended just to lure me to my death. I knew people hated me, but I must admit that I never thought they were this cruel. I knew I was in love when I first saw him. He was simply gorgeous, with his soft smile and kind eyes. He took me the most exciting places, and had lavished me with exotic gifts and precious jewels. When he finally asked me to run away with him on my eighteenth birthday, I nearly fainted with joy.

But Lucas forbade me from meeting him. He said he didn't trust him. Lucas was the mentor Father hired to teach me magic. However, I was so blindly in love that I refused to obey him. I never thought that was the last time I'd ever see that patient old man again. It was a stormy night, and I didn't even suspect him when he led me into a dark room. Immediately I felt magic binding my wrists and ankles and I lost consciousness. They failed to kill me. I had awakened shortly after and had taken them by surprise. I fought my way out, killing every single person on my way. I was so furious that it was a while later till I felt the hollow socket where my left eye should be.

I panicked. I ran back to that place and unseen by anyone, rummaged through the whole building. Finally I found it in a drawer, inside a small velvet box. Carefully cradling the box, I took it home with a wounded heart.

For months, I tried and tried to attach my eye back to no avail. I had heard from a loyal admirer that in a faraway place lived a magician who knew every spell. Desperate for a cure, I traveled to see him. When I reached the old rickety cottage, he came outside, and leaning against his door, he said to me, "What will you give me in return?" before I had even opened my mouth to ask.

"I do not need to give you anything in return. Your job is to fulfill my wish," I said indignantly. He laughed coldly.

"Oh, yes, you will. It's about time you learn that you always have to give in order to gain. However, you shall pay far more than riches."

"I have almost everything. You can choose whatever you want." I was starting dislike this person.

"Oh, but what I want can't be taken from your hoard. I want a part of your magic. For centuries, your family ruled this world, and now that you're the only heir left, it is now time for another powerful family."

"And you think that I'd just hand it over?"

"Seems like you don't have any choice."

65

I paled and sighed in defeat. He sensed that he won the battle, and ordered, "Hold out your hands."

I obliged. Tiny white specks materialized from my hands and floated into his wand. The original dark blue wand turned into a shimmering shade of silver.

"Clear diamond, not bad," he said as he gingerly touched it. "But I had expected you to make me a dark. Pathetic!" he snarled.

I became his apprentice from that day on. I learned that my family had a gene that allowed us to hold twice the capacity of magic than others. People envied us for this, and longed to have the same powers as us. The magician I sought out, whose name I shall not mention, had finally discovered a way to take away my extra powers, leaving me with the normal amount of magic. I also learned that it was the reason why they took my eye. They had hoped to use it as some sort of container, which should have succeeded if I hadn't awoken that fast.

Each day I vowed for revenge. Practicing my magic, training in combat, anything that could make me stronger, I did. The old man had absolutely no idea that I had been flipping through his secret stash of spell books. I wish I could describe he surprise on his face when I finally challenged him. I killed him with one of his own spells. Not that he didn't deserve it, but since then people have said that I've lost my mind and become bloodthirsty.

I do not know if it's true. They say people who are insane often deny the fact that they are. To whomever reading this, please understand that you are holding an invaluable piece of information. I write this message in fear that my eye will be stolen again by unwanted people. If that ever happens, I fear that my loss of sanity might lead to a disastrous path, so I beg you, my friend, present this to me, and pray that it can cure me.

Sincerely, Cynthiana Lorahas

Ryan looked up, shocked. Jessica asked him, "What's wrong?" He wordlessly handed her the letter. After scanning it, Jessica said determinedly, "We have to help her. We need to convince the twins and Lucas that Cynthiana isn't really wicked." With that, she took Ryan's hand and exited the Chamber of Fire.

Ivy screamed. Seppkumis finally got up from the floor, the fury in his eyes gone. He pressed a small tattoo in the shape of the EYE's symbol, a blood-red eye, on his palm.

"As much as I want to let you go, I must call Mistress Cynthiana now," he said regretfully.

"What? Why?" The three of them asked in unison.

"Well, you know how hard it is to get jobs these days, and when you have one like this, you just can't afford to screw up. I'm just following my orders."

Lucas beckoned Travix and Ivy over to him. The walls of magic that once divided them had long dissolved since Nausicaa's death.

"When she comes, get ready," He whispered hoarsely.

"But...... but I don't have any arrows left," Ivy replied worriedly.

"No matter. There are five Color Splashes and the two jars of nymph melodies left. You are in charge of them. Use them wisely."

"Use what wisely?" A melodic voice came from the doorway. The three of them stood, stricken, at the image of Cynthiana right in front of them.

"This stupid door won't open!" Ryan yelled in frustration. After the exited the chamber, they saw a sign labeled "The One and Only Way Out" on a door few feet away from them. Ryan and Jessica went over to it, and for a respectable amount of pounding, kicking, magic, and pleading, the door still wouldn't budge.

"Look! Two more people have fallen into our silly trap!" A gleeful voice cackled behind them. The two of them turned around and immediately wished that they didn't. Standing behind them were apparently the two hags who Lucas had mentioned before they came. They were identical except for their eye color. One had eyes like molten lava, and the other had watery gray-blue ones.

"Humans *are* silly, dearest sister," the blue eyed one spoke. "However, these two are the youngest trespassers I have ever seen in the last three hundred years, even counting the ones who never even made it here, of course. We ought to congratulate them." Her voice was cold and expressionless.

"Mesm, be nice," the red eyed one chided, "Wouldn't want to scare away our supper, right?"

"Quiet, Adrei, you are the one scaring them," Mesm replied, "With your face," she then added.

"We look exactly the same!" Adrei bellowed. Her wrinkled gray skin began to bubble grotesquely and expanded until she was twice her original size. Dirty white hair shot out as if it was electrocuted. Flames came out her now silver-white eyes, burning the beautiful drapings nearby.

"As you can see," Mesm said calmly, "my sister has some sort of temper control problems. I advise you to surrender before things get a bit...... disastrous."

"We mean no harm," Jessica said, "Please kindly let us pass."

"And lose a chance of having human flesh for dinner? I think not," Adrei, who had reverted back to her original size, said as she chuckled.

Ryan stepped forward. "Then we fight. If we win, you let us pass," He suggested.

Adrei and Mesm exchanged a glance and nodded. The one called Adrei even looked excited. "A beauty contest it is!" they declared in unison. "You'll have two hours for preparation. Feel free to us our cosmetics," They gestured to a table that had just magically appeared. "Now if you'll excuse us, it's time for our pedicures!" With that, they immediately disappeared out the door.

Bewildered, Ryan turned to face Jessica. "What just happened?"

"Uh, I think they're challenging us in a beauty contest," Jessica replied.

"But this is easy! Just the sight of them will make the most vicious monster run back crying for their moms. Of course you'll beat them."

"Well, I may look better than both of them," Jessica said superiorly, "but you saw how they're like. Those two will *never* play fair."

"In that case, we'll play the game their way." Ryan said, leading her to the makeup table.

Chapter 8

Cynthiana, in her long red silken gown, her hair stunningly styled, stood in front of the three of them, a sickening smile on her beautiful face. The only thing that seemed out of place was the black eye patch over her eye.

"It's my entire fault. I didn't teach you well enough. If I had been a better teacher, you wouldn't have gone to the bad side, and we all wouldn't be standing here at all," Lucas sighed.

"Don't waste your words on her, Lucas!" Ivy cried. She shouted at Cynthiana, "I want my stone back, and I not be leaving till I get it!"

"Calm down, girl," Cynthiana commanded. She raised her wand, and Ivy quieted instantly. "We don't need to fight, but since you all insist, so let it be that." Holding up her wand, all three of them could feel the aura of fury around her.

"No one will stop me until I get what I wanted."

"Ahhhhhh!" Jessica screamed so loudly that her voice echoed all through the tunnel, and Ryan had to cover his ears. "How could you do this to me?" She turned towards Ryan and started punching him. Despite the hard blows, Ryan could scarcely keep the grin off his face. He had taken Jessica to the cosmetic table, sat her with her back towards the mirror, and started to apply makeup to her face with his best artistic skills, which to say, weren't very good. Through the whole process, Ryan had forbidden Jessica to look in the mirror, and when she finally did, he actually couldn't blame her for screaming that loud.

The Fruity Mixers had already worn off, so Jessica was back to her fair complexion, long wavy black hair, and ice blue eyes. However, Ryan made her eat another one, turning her hair blue and eyes bubble gum pink. Then he added all kinds of makeup on her. Now, Jessica had bright green eyelids, dark purple cheeks, blood red lips, and her hair was up in a crazy hairdo shaped like a beehive. Ryan also added a black beauty spot near the corner of her mouth as the finishing touch.

"If I lose and we end up in the boiling pot as their dinner, I swear I'll kill you again in hell," she threatened.

"Yeah. You sure look scary enough to be a demon," Ryan replied as he dodged her punches.

"Excuse me, sir. You are wanted in the ballroom. Please follow me," a voice rang out. Ryan turned around but didn't see anyone. Then he felt something tugging at his pants and looked down to see a little guy, barely three feet tall, wearing an expensive looking tiny suit.

Jessica gasped. "That's a Sioban Dwarf! They only live in incredibly harsh and cold environments. When it's angry, it fires tiny barbed spears filled with deadly poison much like cnidarians. I have always thought that they were extinct."

"Nidar— what?" Ryan asked, earning an eye-roll from Jessica.

"Pardon me, but it is extremely rude to talk about others as if they are not there," the dwarf said in an elaborate accent. "Will you kindly follow me?"

The dwarf led them into a huge ballroom with a magnificent stage. It was titanium white, and glowed softly under the moonlight that shone thought the floor-to-ceiling windows. The rest of the room, compared to the stage, was rather poorly decorated. The walls were the color of baby diapers in nuclear disasters, and the rug was a nauseous shade of yellowish green.

"We take pride for our works," the dwarf said, pointing at the beautiful stage, "Although we could have done a lot better if the ladies hadn't insisted on decorating most of the ballroom themselves."

"See, Jess, either they're color blind or they have really bad taste," Ryan said. "I'd say you're worth a shot."

A portal popped open, revealing Adrei in a hideous maroon dress completed with lace and ruffles sewn on every layer. She also had a large red polka-dotted bow on top of her head. "I do look rather beautiful in blue, is it not, sister?" she asked.

"I think they're both," Jessica grumbled.

"Wilby, why isn't the girl dressed? I didn't give you permission to live here for nothing. Now start WORKING!" Adrei shouted, her transformation almost finished as she yelled at the poor dwarf.

The dwarf scurried over and bowed. "Of course, milady. I do not know if this is a suitable time to mention this, but, about the pay raise— "

"Do we have to repeat ourselves, Wilby? Off to work," Mesm said, her voice cold. Sensing her anger, the dwarf quickly led Jessica through another door. The blue eyed hag had on a dress that was even more bizarre. It had a wild jungle-ish flower print, browns and greens covering most of her dress. There was a vivid neon green vine-like belt around her waist, and a huge bright hibiscus was fastened above her shoulder. A plastic boa constrictor was wrapped around her neck like a scarf. Adrei saw Mesm's outfit and shrieked, "You're prettier than me!"

"No, you're prettier!" Mesm cried, seeing Adrei for the first time.

"Whoa, hold your horses, girls, "A hooded figure strolled into the ballroom, saying, "If I remember correctly, I am the judge of the contest, and I decide who's the prettiest. You are welcome to fight afterwards, but please don't begin before the pageant's even started."

"Aladar," Mesm spat in disdain. "Arrogant as usual."

Aladar chuckled. "And where's our other contestant? I heard that she's rather beautiful. Anyone know where she is? Anyone?" He stopped for a minute then sighed. "Very well. We'll start without her."

"There's no freaking way I'm wearing that," Jessica muttered. "Or that," she added, glancing at a furry white gown with a huge pink bow on the bosom. "None of the sizes even fit. And I have absolutely no idea when the contest will start." She sighed and sat down on the mountain of dresses that were left in a mess after the hags had chosen their outfits. Apparently the dwarf had led her to the world's largest walk-in closet. She had washed off the hideous makeup Ryan applied in the nearby bathroom, and to her relief she also managed to change back her appearance.

What to wear....Seems like she couldn't find a single normal dress out of thousands.

Then she caught her eye on some large black plastic bags that were apparently used for keeping dresses clean.

"Alright, then," she said, grabbing a pair of scissors and a box of sewing tools, "it's improvising time."

"Come on, where are you, Jessica? Please be here in time for your turn, okay?" Ryan prayed.

71

"Welcome, ladies, gentlemen, and magical creatures of all sorts, to the beauty pageant of Volcano Acrakk! I shall explain the rules briefly. As you can see, we have our lovely red carpet in front of our wonderful stage. Contestants will walk down the carpet, go up the stage, and stand in your most striking poses," Aladar, who seemed to be the host as well as the judge, announced gleefully to the audience, which included of Ryan, Wilby, and a few other creatures.

"The judge, which of course is me, will score your looks as you go down the runway. Points will be taken off because of fighting, arguing, or jealousy. And now, without further ado, shall we?" Aladar asked, with a graceful wave of his hand.

Mesm went first. She stumbled most of her way down the carpet, but she managed to keep a bright smile on her face, as if it didn't bother her much. Waving her plastic snake around, Mesm almost tripped again when she went onstage. However, she seemed unfazed by it, and struck an outrageous pose, her back almost bended in ninety degrees, both of her hands curled into fists beneath her chin, and pouted her lips.

"Hey! I had planned to use that pose too! You stole it from me!" Adrei yelled angrily.

"Did not."

"Did too."

"Did not."

"Did too."

"Did too."

"Did not."

"Correct! I did NOT steal your idea!" Mesm said triumphantly.

"You tricked me!" Adrei spat as her face began to bubble once more. She ran onstage and shoved Mesm, sending her flying to the carpet.

"Enough!" Aladar shouted. "I am deeply disappointed in both of you girls. Like I said before, I will deduct points because of your behavior. Now stand still like a decent lady!"

"They're ladies?" Ryan muttered.

"Tell me about it," Wilby, sitting beside him, muttered back.

Aladar rose from his chair and led Mesm down the stage. "Adrei, your turn," he said.

Adrei smiled and shot a look at Mesm, who was sitting grumpily in a chair. "Wait till you see MY pose!" she said. She walked to the beginning of the red carpet and began her show. Adrei pranced down the carpet, her face bubbling revoltingly the whole time. She was actually quite graceful compared to Mesm, but she, too, tripped while going up the stage.

"Hey! You're copying....." Mesm started to cry out, but was silenced by a glare from Aladar. Seeing the glare, Ryan vowed never to get on Aladar's bad side, because if looks could kill, the glare would've vaporized him right on the spot.

Adrei rounded off her turn with a flourish, putting her hands under her chin like a flower and blinked her eyes. Her legs were crossed, and Ryan wanted to throw up when he saw that.

"Does she really think that the pose is suitable for her? I mean, I won't mind other girls doing that, but the sight of her gives me nightmares," Ryan whispered to Wilby.

"Our ladies think that they are very sweet and beautiful, so whenever they see something that is cute, they try it out in themselves whether it fits them or not," Wilby answered.

"Well, it definitely does NOT fit," Ryan muttered. Wilby nodded in agreement.

Aladar clapped his hands. "Alright, Adrei, you're done," he said. "Time for our last contestant." He looked around the room and frowned. "Will someone kindly tell me where she is?"

Cynthiana smoothed her luxurious golden hair. "I am a good girl. I am a good girl. I am a good girl......"she chanted absentmindedly. Her single jade green eye was hollow.

"Be she crazy?" Ivy whispered to Travix.

"Quiet," he replied.

"You don't have to do this, my dear," Lucas said aloud. "I— "

"He left me," Cynthiana interrupted. "And he did *this*," she pointed at her eye patch, "to me. Now he's going to pay for it."

"*He* did that to you? I thought—"

"I thought I killed them all," she said, her voice wavering, "but I knew he was not there. He fled, like a coward. I can feel it. "Her voice was then filled with anger, "I vowed to be a good girl, to only kill the ones that deserved to die. But it's so hard that it's not fair! Everyone kept getting in the way. I *am* a good girl, aren't I?" She fixed her eye on Lucas, as if daring him to disagree.

"She's completely mental, but she's dangerous. What should we—" Travix whispered to Lucas.

"Stop whispering!" Cynthiana cried. "Bind!" Black metal chains snaked around their bodies, trapping and forcing them on their knees.

Travix shouted, "Loosen!" The chains dropped, and the second they were free, he commanded the chains to attack Cynthiana, who deflected it easily. The same time, Ivy ran to her bag and started fumbling with the lid of the orange melody jar. Lucas, however, was still kneeling in shock, staring at Cynthiana as if he didn't know her anymore.

Travix pulled Lucas up just in time as a bolt of pure energy blasted down where Lucas previously sat. The old man seemed to have lost all signs of fighting back, and that worried Travix. He sneaked a small glance at his sister, quickly deciding to put Lucas as his priority. Ivy would just have to manage on her own.

Oh, if you just knew, the power you have over me........ Obnoxious, loud rock music with screaming electric guitars blasted out from behind Travix. He turned around to look at Ivy, who had succeeded in opening the jar. There was an orange aura surrounding her, and she gave off a golden glow as if bathed in sunlight. White swirls were coming out of Ivy's fingertips. She raised her hands and pointed them directly towards Cynthiana. Tendrils of the white magic shot towards Cynthiana, heading for her head. They entered through the scalp and disappeared inside.

"You now have unlimited power over me," Cynthiana said in a flat voice, her eyes blank.

"Stop it. Stop everything you have done already. Forget all about your past, forget about revenge. Please, Cynthiana." Ivy pleaded.

Cynthiana nodded at first, but then she shook her head, as if trying to get rid of a bad thought. Lucas, who had finally come to his senses by that time, shouted, "Ivy, she's coming out of it! Push her harder!" Another blast of white magic went into Cynthiana's mind. Ivy kept on pleading, yet Cynthiana always seemed to struggle against her.

"Ivy's doing a great job, but she is still no match for Cynthiana, even with the melody helping her. Eventually, Cynthiana will either overpower her, or the melody will wear off, depending on what happens first. You and I better get ready." Travix nodded, not taking his eyes off his sister.

Cynthiana was fighting hard to escape the magic to no avail. Every time she became unfazed. Ivy pointed her hands toward Cynthiana again. Even though Ivy seemed to have the upper hand, Travix could see that her willpower was crumbling, and she didn't have much energy left. As he watched, the orange glow around her began to get dimmer and dimmer........

Ryan was starting to get jumpy when Aladar announced that if Jessica was not present within ten minutes, she would be disqualified, so he almost cried with joy when he finally heard her familiar voice. However, the boy lost his ability to speak one he took in the sight of her.

Jessica managed to change her appearance back and wash away his poorly done makeup. Her long raven locks hung loosely and a single red rose adorned her face, making her already fair skin milky white in contrast. She wore a simple black dress that seemed to float around her knees and a pair of ballet flats. Dark ribbons laced around her left arm, adding grace and elegance. A deep red jewel shone bewitchingly under the moonlight on her slender finger, which Ryan realized was the ruby of her necklace. In short, she was breathtaking.

A pinkish hue rose to her cheeks. "I couldn't find anything to wear, so I, uh, whipped this up," she whispered as she fumbled with her dress. Ryan noticed that the material was oddly, plastic. No wonder it floated.

"Took you long enough," he retorted, finally finding his voice.

Jessica glared. "You have no idea how hard I—"

"Ahem," Aladar said. "If you don't mind, will you go onstage and make a pretty pose?"

"Of c-course!" Jessica stammered and walked along the red carpet, ignoring Ryan's snickers.

She made her way upstage, blushed, and twirled. The crowd cheered loudly, unaware that Adrei and Mesm were seething in jealousy.

"Thank you, Jessica. That is quite a dress. Please take a seat." Aladar said, beaming at Jessica.

Once again, the girl turned bright red, and sat down next to Ryan.

"Hey! The ribbons are from my blue sequined mini skirt! You cut them off!" Mesm suddenly screamed, pointing an accusing finger at her.

"Ha ha ha....." Adrei laughed at her sister's misfortune, then she shrieked, "The laces are from my ruffle front party dress! You little thief!"

75

"It doesn't matter," Mesm said, regaining her cool facade. "I will win the contest in the end."

"I beg to differ, sister. The winner will be ME!" Adrei said smugly.

Aladar strolled to the stage and adjusted his clothes. "Well, the results are in, ladies. The winner is—" he paused dramatically, then rolled his eyes as if he couldn't believe he actually had to announce it, "of course it's our lovely Jessica," he muttered.

"I knew— wait— WHAT?" Adrei and Mesm cried in unison.

"No!" The hags yelled together. "It simply can't be her!"

"And may I ask why is that?" Aladar asked, rolling his eyes.

"Cause we're prettier, that's why!" They cried, "Stop talking like me!"

Jessica stayed frozen in her seat, as if in a trance, until Ryan shook her and said, "Hello, Miss Beauty Queen, but we have a task to do, remember?"

"Oh, right. Let's go then. Just let me get changed." As they stood up, Mesm ran in front of them and growled in their faces, "You're not going anywhere!"

"Yeah! No one ever wins the beauty pageant except for us!" Adrei chimed in.

Ryan looked at Jessica. "Uh oh," he said.

Cynthiana felt dazed. Some kind of energy was controlling her mind, making her think about giving up revenge. The worst thing was, she actually wanted to do it. She reminded herself to focus, and though about her missing eye, the one exchanged for her life, locked safely in a totally safe box, hidden in a place with the most enchantments. As she thought, her mind became clear enough to see that controlling her was that girl, Iris, or whatever her name was. That brat had found a jar of nymph melody and somehow managed to succumb her. She smiled and raised her hand, preparing to strike.

"Here we go again," Aladar sighed. "But I do have to say that I actually enjoy it. Alright, all magical creatures out! It's show time!"

Wilby gazed sympathetically at Ryan and mouthed "Good luck!" Then he followed the other creatures out of the chamber.

"Um, what's going on?" Jessica asked nervously, inching towards Ryan.

"Ha! You think that we'd let you get away with this?" Adrei cried. She had already resumed her original scary form, fire shooting out of her eyes at them. A heavy mace was held in her hands. However this time Ryan was ready. He pulled out Mirroride and stabbed Adrei hard in the foot. She wailed in pain, allowing Jessica to have a split-second advantage and send a blast of purple energy that shocked Adrei back ten feet.

A giddy voice echoed through the room. "Awesome! Now keep on fighting! As you can see, Mr. Ryan and Miss Jessica have taken on the challenge and are doing their best to stay alive. Will they make it? Keep watching for more details!"

Ryan looked up to see a shiny silver platform rising from the ground, and the person standing on it, looking very satisfied with himself, was Aladar. He was shouting into a sparkly jewel encrusted microphone.

Ryan turned to Jessica, bewildered, "This is being televised?"

"Oh, yes! It gets top reviews every time and the best part is always when we kill you!" Mesm laughed and rushed towards him, jaws bared. Ryan sidestepped and counter attacked with his sword, engaging himself in battle.

Meanwhile, Jessica had taken on Adrei and was conquering bolts of water from her wand and shooting them towards Adrei every time the hag spouted fire. Adrei was soaked, and wisps of smoke came out of her eyes.

"Die! You miserable little—" Mesm's cry was cut down abruptly, for Ryan had successfully slammed the hilt of his sword onto her stomach, causing her to stagger backwards and pant for her momentarily loss of breath.

"Looks like Mr. Ryan here got a lucky blow, folks." Aladar's voice rang out.

"You're really annoying, you know that?" was Jessica's reply. She had just dodged Adrei's blow and was currently trying to find the energy to summon her magic back.

Aladar shrugged indifferently. With a glance at his silver pocket watch, he called out, "Okay, time out! Warm up's over! I will now declare the rules of this challenge. I said 'time out' Mesm! You too, Adrei!" He sighed in defeat. With one swift movement he whipped away his cloak, finally revealing his face. He was actually pretty good-looking, with dark brown hair and amber eyes sparkling with mischief. He smirked, and they could see a trail of black symbols snaking down his forehead to his left cheek, which stood out in contrast to his pale skin. When he snapped his fingers, a pair of gigantic wings sprouted from his back.

"You're... you're a ..." Jessica tried to speak but stumbled helplessly with her words.

"Yes, yes. Calm down. No pictures please." Aladar said as a very cocky grin spread across his face. "People call our species Maedella, which by the way, means 'a pile of feathers', so you can see that I'm not all that thrilled to reveal my identity. Unfortunately, the name of my species is the trigger word for this to appear." He held out his right palm and a crystal floated above it, glowing in a faint golden light.

"The Maedell Crystal," Jessica breathed out. "I can't believe I'm actually seeing it with my own eyes.

"Yeah, it's a useful thingy," he said casually.

"Useful thingy? The crystal is practically— "

"Well, enough talking about me." He flashed a seductive smile to one of the cameras on the ceiling. "Though I'd be more than happy if one of you pretty ladies call this number."

"What the heck is he saying? And why do you seem to understand what he's talking about?" Ryan asked Jessica.

"The Maedella is a kind of angel-demon hybrid. They have the appearances of an angel, but deep down they are just plain evil, and are always trying to take advantages of people. Just keep one thing in mind: Don't believe or really listen to what Aladar says, because it's mainly just him showing off or playing tricks with your mind."

"What about that crystal?"

"The Maedell Crystal is one of the most powerful tools of magic, and only the Maedella have it. It's a pity they only use it to show off instead of doing some good to the world. The Maedella are one of the few magical creatures that are able to do magic."

"Anyhow," Aladar interrupted, "there's only one major rule. I hereby declare, the first person to yield will be kicked out of the game. You can't just walk off, either. You have to say loudly and clearly, 'I yield'. Now repeat after me. 'I YIELD'."

"That's just stupid!" Jessica said out loud. "Cut the theatrics, all right?"

"Well, Miss Jessica certainly has spunk. Okay then, if you refuse to repeat, we'll start right now, disregarding the proper rules. When the gong rings, start! Ready?" He struck a gong that appeared beside him, and the sound echoed across the room, making the walls and floor vibrate. Ryan was recovering from the weird sensation when he felt the temperature rapidly increase in front of him and heard a sizzling sound coming from the T-shirt he was wearing. Adrei had shot a blast of fire onto his stomach. Without his fireproof abilities, Ryan would probably die on the spot. The blast brought back his concentration, and he scanned the room. What he saw made him gasp in horror.

Mesm had also transformed, and was even more terrifying than Adrei. She, too, had doubled in size, but that was the only similarity.

Her hair floated and swirled ghostly around her head as if underwater, and revolting dark blue blotches covered her body. But the most terrifying part was her mouth. Yellow-green droplets were continuously dripping down, and the floor sizzled where the drops fell.

He glanced at Jessica, who was staring wide-eyed at the display, until realization dawned her and she let out a small squeak.

"Come on! The audience is waiting! Or are you too shocked to move?" Aladar taunted. He was soaring around the room, looking bored. "You know the rules. Five minutes of not moving, and I'll let one of the monsters out!"

"Rules?! You didn't say anything about rules!" Jessica shrieked as she ducked Mesm's kick at the last second. A few strands of her hair near her face were singed by the acid-spitting maniac attacking her, and she felt like she was losing it.

"Yes I did," Aladar calmly replied. "And I quote, 'if you refuse to repeat, we'll start right now, disregarding the rules'. Ha ha. Your loss." Smirking, the dark haired man held out the crystal. A portal appeared almost immediately and a cute little monster wobbled out. It was shaped like a cherry, and only reached Ryan's knee. However, there was a silver wire waving on top of its head, making its full length more than five feet. The monster was neon red, with electric blue eyes and a small mouth. There was a gold starburst shaped ball of electricity on top of the silver wire.

"I just love this Crystal!" Aladar exclaimed. "It always chooses the most appropriate monster in each situation. In this case, I hope you enjoy being fried, Miss Jessica!"

"Aww, it's so cute!" Ryan said. However, he regretted his words a split-second later. The little monster's circle feet allowed it to zoom around the room like a demon on wheels, and the silver wire kept slapping people or firing bolts of electricity through the starburst. Static sounds came out of its mouth in a rhythmic pattern, as if it was singing happily in its own language.

It slapped Jessica's back, making her jump three feet in the air.

"Ho! Looks like Miss Jessica got what she deserved. It hurts a lot, right?" Aladar flew above her, patted her hair, and soared away, making a face at Jessica. Ryan started to laugh, but when she glared at him and asked, "Would you like to be electrocuted by a ten thousand volt wire?" he shut up immediately. Good thing he did, because the little devil was heading right towards him.

It stared at him with its wide set eyes, curiosity swimming in those blue depths. The monster seemed to be entranced with his blond hair, and it glanced up at its own golden starburst. A huge smile formed across his face as it rushed to him.

"Family!" it squealed in delight, tackling him in an electrifying bear hug.

"Aghhhh!" Ryan remembered the time he stuck the hand of his toy robot into an electric socket in third grade. The felling was the same, except that the pain was multiplied a thousand times. He felt his heart beating wildly, and his legs, especially at the places where the monster hugged him, were shaking like crazy.

He was starting to see stars when the pain finally ended and he collapsed on the floor with a thump. Adrei had tried to brain him with her mace but she slipped because of the water Jessica summoned earlier, and ended bashing the monster away instead.

The little monster became unconscious, reduced into a ball of white light, and flew into Aladar's crystal.

"Hmmp. I thought the Volter Dwarf would last a little bit longer, but apparently I was wrong, folks. Well, one down and three more to go!" came Aladar's cheerful voice. At the sound of him, Jessica had the urge to pull off his wings.

Mentally cursing, she surveyed their situation. Adrei was not much of a threat since she couldn't use fire anymore, and her mace had severed in half. However, her supreme strength was still quite a problem. Mesm preferred long distance attacks, such as firing darts dipped in acid from her crossbow, which she did at Ryan just then. He ducked to avoid it, and the dart accidentally hit Aladar's shiny white shoes. Once the acid made connection with the shoes, they started to melt.

"Do you know how much these custom-made, unicorn leather, formal occasion shoes cost? This is the fifty-seventh pair you've ruined, Mesm! Penalty for the hags! Either Mr. Ryan or Miss Jessica may have a choice to torture the hags for five minutes in whatever way they like. Also," He yelled into the microphone, "I think that I'm going to need another pair of shoes, since the acid is starting to make its way though my body. Donators are welcome! Send your little gifts to Volcano Acrakk!"

"No fair!" Adrei cried. "The last time you said that, we got tangled with vines until we looked like a pair of green mummies with leaves! Aladar, you just want a chance to get shoes again. Stop playing dirty tricks!"

"You are making me very angry now, Adrei. Are you trying to test my temper like you did to me last time? The five minutes of attacking hags will begin in one minute. Please decide whether Mr. Ryan or Miss Jessica will be doing the dirty work. Meanwhile, Adrei and Mesm will only be allowed to attack with their weapons, without any fire or acid."

Ryan looked at Jessica. "Are you going to fight them?" he asked. Jessica said, "They'll only be able to use weapons, which means it will be hand-to-hand combat. My magic won't be any use in this situation. You have your sword, so you should go." Ryan was hesitating, but she pushed him gently towards the center of the room.

"Looks like Mr. Ryan is going to take them! What are the odds so he can win?"

Ryan walked slowly towards Adrei and Mesm, Mirroride clutched tightly in his hand.

"The five minutes officially start now!" Aladar said cheerfully. "Oh, I almost forgot. While Mr. Ryan is fighting Adrei and Mesm, we can't just let Miss Jessica stand in a corner biting her fingernails, can we? Of course not! We will now be releasing another one of our little pets for her to play with. Lucky you!"

Ryan, too busy listening to Aladar, earned a blow at his head from Mesm. However, his fighting instincts kicked in, and he stabbed her in the stomach with Mirroride. He then kicked Adrei, who was sneaking up from behind him. Both of them winced, but kept on fighting. Mesm glared at Ryan with her bloodshot eyes and growled, "No warrior has ever bested me before. You'll never get out of here alive."

"Yeah, like that'll happen," Ryan taunted and blocked an arrow from her with Mirroride.

"Three minutes left for Mr. Ryan! Ooh, dangerous choice, Miss Jessica! The Rockin' Slime Golem sure doesn't like to be melted into a puddle! Watch out!" Aladar's shrill voice sounded throughout the room.

Ryan sneaked a glance at Jessica. She was fighting a vaguely humanoid, bright orange blob of slime. It kept wiggling, and whenever it touched Jessica, loud screaming rock music played, almost making their ears burst.

"For the viewers' information, the Rockin' Slime Golem is an amazing artist. Once it grabs hold of you, you turn into a jello sculpture with every detail intact. Magnificent, isn't it?"

Ryan stared at Jessica distractedly. How could she ever defeat that by herself? The monster was now a puddle, but it was still making ear-splitting music, and would probably turn Jessica into a wiggly, edible sculpture that would be devoured by the hags after the fight as a special treat if she wasn't careful enough.

However, Ryan still had his own dilemma. Both hags were wounded, but they still had energy to fight back. He had to defeat them before the five minutes ended.

"Ryan, catch!" Jessica screamed. She tossed something into the air, and he caught it instinctively.

It was one of the two jars they bought at the Grand Taske Market. The one with translucent fuchsia bubbles floating on top of the periwinkle violet surface. Grimacing, he twisted open the lid.

Guitar chords melodically penetrated through the walls, filling the whole chamber with soft music. A cloud of baby pink mist surrounded the hags, temporarily blocking his view.

On the other hand, the second the Rockin' Slime Golem heard the music, it cooed and immediately stopped singing and attacking Jessica. The long-haired girl took the opportunity to imprison it in her water bottle.

"Oh my, oh my! Looks like our little beauty queen defeated the Slime Golem! Excellent job! But what exactly has Mr. Ryan done? What's with the pink smoke? Is it possible that the mighty warrior loves the color pink? Keep watching, folks!" Aladar said in mock surprise. With a wave of his hand, Jessica's water bottle flew into his crystal.

"Hey! Give it back!" Jessica demanded.

"Uh uh uh. I simply can't lose one of my precious little mon –" His jaw dropped.

Jessica turned around. The pink fog had cleared, and it revealed—

A smoking hot red head and a stunningly pretty petite girl.

The auburn haired girl managed to look both willowy and curvy, with long slender legs and a slim waist. Her hair was curled and went past her shoulders like liquid copper. Her eyes, those beautiful forest green jewels, were guaranteed to hold men mesmerized.

The petite girl was equally gorgeous, if not more. She had short light brown hair with bangs that hung neatly just below her eyebrows. Long lashes framed her cerulean eyes, and she had full, luscious lips.

The taller girl wore a strapless salmon colored dress that came to her ankle, but there was a slit on the side and it showed off her creamy legs. The shorter girl had on a blue satin dress that fell above her knees. It matched perfectly with the color of her eyes and was held together at her back with white criss-crossed ribbons.

Both girls scowled. "What have you done to me, you pathetic little –" The green-eyed girl then clutched her throat in horror. "What happened to my voice?"

"Adrei?" the blue-eyed girl gasped. Her voice was also soft and melodic, similar to the other girl. She rubbed her eyes, trying to register what had happened.

"My skin! My beautiful wrinkly gray skin! My hair! My carefully styled stringy white hair! My body! My perfect barrel-shaped figure! Aghhhhhh!" she broke into hysterics, eyes wide in unbelievement.

Aladar was having a hard time breathing. The two women in front of him were so breathtakingly beautiful that all he could hear was the wild thumping of his heart, the roaring of blood in his ears, and the slight dizziness in his head. Oh how he longed to push them to the wall, start tearing off their— Well, some things are better left unsaid. He quickly hid his thoughts by looking as innocent as possible. "Where have our hags gone? And who are these pretty young ladies?"

"Oh, shut up, Aladar," the green-eyed girl, Adrei, growled.

Mesm, on the other hand, looked like she was about to faint. The girl lost all signs of her previous cool and collected composure, and was now grasping her sister's right arm with trembling hands like there was no tomorrow. "Change us back! Oh please change us back! I'll do anything you want! Just change us back!" Crocodile tears were brimming in her eyes, and Ryan had to admit that she sounded pretty convincing.

Jessica shot him a glare, and he immediately snapped out of it.

"Um, I'm sorry that you became beautiful? But I don't know how to change you guys back. I'm really, er, sorry." He said.

"Stop talking nonsense to him, sister dear. Don't forget that we still have one more trick up our sleeves," Adrei smirked and clapped her hands. A bunch of twinkling lights flew in and Adrei whispered something to them. Blinking as if they understood what she said, they then flew away.

Suddenly the double doors flew open and a figure stumbled in. Ryan could vaguely see that it was a woman, with wild white hair standing up. There was a bump on her nose and her skin was a nauseous green. When she came closer, he heard her screaming, "I'm a well known fortune teller from Taske, and I demand you to let me go! I'm warning you, there is a whole truckload of admirers back home, especially one with dark diamond magic!" The swarm of lights was blocking her way back, forcing her to go forward.

"Evelynda! You're here!" Ryan and Jessica exclaimed.

"Oh, finally!" She let out an exasperated sigh. "After I fell into the hole, I met the two hags, and they dared to try and make me their sister once they caught sight of me! Things were already ugly, but when I accidentally looked into my Kuloo, I saw that a big change would happen to them. These two were particularly unpleasant after hearing the news, especially the crazy one."

"Who are you calling crazy? Shut up and be a good hostage!" Adrei shouted.

"I never said it was you," Evelynda retorted. "Anyway, so I was forced to stay inside a small room after that, and just then I was summoned here and saw you two. Well, it seems that I was right about the big change, so we can go to help the others now!"

"Certainly, that's exactly what we should do!" agreed Aladar, who was itching to have alone time with Adrei and Mesm. "Mr. Ryan has done something that has never happened before. He has successfully defeated our monsters and transformed our ladies into lovely girls. Miss Jessica, as much as I don't like her, has also proved herself worthy. I hereby declare you the first ever winners, and are granted safe access through Volcano Acrakk!"

"Awesome! Now let's go!" Ryan said.

Jessica made a portal again, and they stepped through it, leaving Adrei and Mesm howling in protest.

Chapter 9

Travix's heart pounded. He looked frantically for a way out, even though he was sure there were none. They were losing, the battle and hope. Cynthiana broke the mind controlling spell and stunned Ivy as soon as she gained control of herself. Now his little sister was collapsed on the floor, and Lucas couldn't wake her, not even with magic. Moreover, they were all weak, tired, and unable to fight back.

Cynthiana said, "Surrender. You can help me expand the EYE, and we can become the most powerful group ever. You will never have to work hard again. You can live a luxurious life just like mine." Even though her voice still had a commanding tone in it, her face, too, had a weary look to it.

Travix had to admit that she was pretty convincing, and there was no way he and Lucas could defeat her. Even though the old man had a higher level of magic than Cynthiana, his age got in the ways of his doings. However, just as Travix opened his mouth to bargain, make a witty remark, anything to distract Cynthiana, a purple portal appeared between them. Ryan, Jessica, and Evelynda, who had resumed her original form, came out of it.

"You dare request reinforcements?" Cynthiana snarled. Before waiting for an answer, she gave a shrill whistle. Something came thundering through the hall, something big and heavy. A huge red cow with sharp black horns came towards them. Ryan could feel his whole body trembling and started to get light-headed. "That's.... that's the..." he couldn't bring himself to say the word "cow". "It...was in a dream you sent me."

"Yes, she's my Daisy," Cynthiana answered, stroking the cow's bright red fur. Daisy looked straight at Ryan and mooed loudly, horns pointed directly at him. Ryan started to remember a hazy memory of him when he was five, while a cow walked around him with a pair of pants and underwear in its mouth.

Ryan muttered, "No Cows," then slowly fell to the floor, losing consciousness. A jar of melodies, the one like a mug of hot chocolate that was in his hands, fell and crashed.

A sweet voice rebounded through the circular hallway, mixing with a faint aroma of chocolate. The soothing melody of a lullaby seemed to have a magical calming effect, every note reminding them of past memories, the nice ones that gave them comfort.

Soon every single person in the hallway was drifting to sleep, even Cynthiana, though she kept on struggling to stay awake. She was just about to surrender and collapse on the Sandman's lap when purple flames appeared. The portal stretched and a figure stepped though. He was clad from head to toe in black, with dark eyes and hair contrasting the unhealthy paleness of his skin. Seeing him, Cynthiana's eye immediately went wide open as she deftly made her way towards him.

"Well, well. Wakey wakey, sleepy heads. Don't you dare sleep through my performance," he said in an all too familiar voice.

Jessica was suddenly awake. "Cee?" she said in disbelief. Anger and looks of betrayal contorted her face. She shook her head wildly, as if trying to deny the fact that her most trusted friend and teacher was the man in front of her.

"My apologies, sweetheart. However, you must know that what I am doing is inevitable," he replied. An ivory wand appeared in his hand. With a flick of his wrist, Jessica went crashing into the walls.

Ryan and the others had woken just in time to see the scene. Ryan ran to her and helped her on her feet, while Lucas and Travix went into battle stance. Ivy, who had no arrows left, was now acting as Evelynda's protector.

"Now, don't get too excited," he said. "Everyone gets a part in this play. There's absolutely no need to fight."

"A play? What play?" Cynthiana demanded. She placed a hand on his shoulder, making him face her.

A look of distaste crossed his face. "Don't. Touch. Me." He said, disgust evident in his tone. He sneered and waved his wand, and a white flash temporarily blinded them. When they could finally regain their vision, they found themselves in a completely different place.

"Funny how a simple dimension spell can shock you," he said. "I had create a new one, since we wouldn't want people running away before their acts were over. Still, I can't afford to take any chances. So I'm deeply sorry that I have to do this." Another wave of his wand and a glowing ball of energy enveloped them all, except for himself. It became a transparent shell, trapping them in it.

The ones who could perform magic tried to break through, but to no avail. Cee smirked. "You cannot harm it, especially not with your stupid sword, boy," he added, seeing that Ryan was trying to hack it with Mirroride. "You do know I'm even more powerful than all of you combined, right?" His eyes lit up as he saw their reactions, whether anger or shock.

"I order you to explain what is happening," Cynthiana seethed. "I will not tolerate betrayals. And you certainly cannot be stronger than me!"

Cee threw a glance over his shoulder where she was standing. "I did not betray you. This is exactly how it should have happened. Actually, it should have happened ages ago. I merely delayed it. But my plans always work, no doubting that. After all, a *Lorahas's* plan is flawless. Isn't it?" He raised his eyebrows at Cynthiana, as if waiting to see her fully comprehend the meaning of his words.

But he was disappointed. "Don't you use my family's phrase, you traitor," she said coldly. With that, she charged, casting a blast of lightning to him, which the latter easily dodged.

"Puppets are meant to be controlled. Nothing can change that." Cee smiled as he tore something off of his face. It was a mask, one of those gruesome ones made to look exactly like a real person. The face under it was more than horrible, but under all the frightening scars, they could see the same jade green eyes with flecks of gold around the pupil.

Cynthiana's only eye widened. "You... have the Lorahas eyes. But that can't be true. I'm an only child."

"Is that so, little sister?" Cee asked, a mocking tone in his voice. Cynthiana flinched at the term, but stood her ground, glaring at her so-called brother. "Explain yourself," she commanded.

"Oh, yes, I will come to my sorrowful story in a minute. However, beforehand I must clarify that I certainly am a Lorahas. And now, I shall start my story, one about my pitiful life." Cee smiled malevolently. Ryan could distinctively see the family resemblance between Cynthiana and Cee. While the smile on Cynthiana looked sinister enough, Cee's expression took evil up another level.

"I was the heir to all of the Lorahas wealth and magic. I could have had everything, if it wasn't for you!" Cee pointed a finger at Cynthiana, quivering in anger.

"After you were born, our parents, who had always wanted a girl, started to focus all on you. I have to admit; at first I quite liked you, with your adorable blond curls and bright eyes like me. However, with you around, everyone forgot about me. I started to be unloved. I lost all the attention I had to begin with, only having to give it all to you. Nothing I did, no matter how amazing, was even acceptable compared to the small silly actions of yours."

"I started to grow sullen and began to detest you. I tried everything I could to harm you and get you out of my way. But you were always protected, with someone there to defend you, even if you deserved it. They separated us in order to keep you safe and I was sent to a school far away. That was when I learned about why you were so loved. Our parents were cruel. Just because I didn't have our family's special gift, twice the capacity of magic than others,

they ignored me. You had the gift, and that was why you got all the attention!"
Cee's voice started to rise, almost as if he was reaching a breaking point.

"I vowed to make you pay. I sent spies after you and schemed of ways to dispose of you. You do remember your eighteenth birthday, correct?" At this question, Cynthiana paled and raised a hand to her mouth. She nodded, almost imperceptibly.

"Oh yes, I was behind that all. We planned it together. The scheme would have worked, if only you hadn't woken up at the wrong moment. Which would've been a big shame, but there were other ways. Because you never knew me, it was quite easy to get a position near you and follow your every move. I was a very good actor, always giving you the best advice and obeying your every command on the surface. On the inside, however, my notions never stopped. Who recommended you to go that old magician? I did, in hopes that you would lose half of your magic and become normal, which was just as I predicted. The same time, I worked my way towards power inside of Daske. After a year of hard work, I was given the title of 'Most Trusted Advisor' and was granted access to the castle as I liked. The purple orb of energy in the prophecy room has always been a big help to me, giving me more and more magical energy, until now I have more magic than any living person!" He laughed dryly.

"Anyway, even though it took a long time, my plans are finally reaching their destination. I will regain everything that once was mine, and you, Cynthiana Lorahas, will be sorry that you were ever alive!"

Deafening silence replied him.

Cynthiana stared at him, her eye blank. "But......" She staggered backwards, almost bumping into Ryan.

"Fascinating story of yours, man. Please, you're such an attention grabber. You're not the only person ignored by parents, you know. I am like the very definition of a neglected child. Somehow I survived without being all evil and crazy like you," Ryan crossed his arms in front of his chest.

That seemed to stun him. "You'll have time for your snarky remarks later, boy. I'm not done yet. Every single one of you will have to be broken, either mentally or physically. We'll start with you first, little princess. Whether you like it or not, you are pretty similar to my darling sister. Bathed in love till this day and completely spoiled. Don't look at me that way, you know you are. And that is precisely the reason why I chose Daske to build my forces. So I—"

"I don't want to hear you talk about myself." Jessica spat.

He ignored her and continued, "So I made up this silly name Cee and started to work in the castle as a servant. Imagine this— the great Claym Lorahas— working as a mere kitchen boy! At least I got one family trait that's useful— patience. I crawled my way up, but then your parents got that insane idea that I can teach you the ways of magic. And I did, but not before murdering them. You became quieter and I gained power. That's like killing two birds with one stone. Brilliant, right?"

Jessica's eyes went blank just like Cynthiana's. Claym laughed. He was enjoying this, drinking up every ounce of energy that seemed to be pouring out of her like a tidal wave.

"And you two," he began to address Ivy and Travix. "I don't need to repeat the unfortunate fate of your tribe, yes? The Lorahas have always supported the Volcrast tribe. How would I find out about your life stones if not? I must admit that they are very useful to me, and that's why I decide to add you into my little play.

"What do you mean by saying our life stones are useful to you? As far as I can remember, Cynthiana has always taken control of them." Travix asked, trying hard not to let his anger get the best of him.

"Oh, so that's how you think! How naive! For your answer, in order to get the effect I wanted, I had to break up your tribe. Yet, to avoid suspicion, I needed another person to do the dirty work for me. So, as Cynthiana's faithful assistant, I manipulated her into destroying the Volcrast tribe under the notion that it would do the EYE good. Meanwhile, I lounged in my office, waiting for the result that was all for my benefit!"

Cynthiana widened her eye while the twins both had looks of distaste and outrage.

"Oh, yes. That is exactly what I did. Then, the two of you were captured and brought to the EYE as apprentices under Cynthiana. Yet, she treated you badly, lighting the spark of revenge inside your hearts. You vowed to overturn her and take control someday. What you didn't know is that the person really behind it all was me! What will you do now? Quite a twist, isn't it?" Claym said dramatically, arms spread wide as he pictured.

"You...you planned all that?" Travix uttered through clenched teeth.

"Give us back our stones! You meanie!" Ivy demanded.

Claym sighed. "No. You got it all wrong! You were supposed to express the lost in your heart," he said to Travix. "And you," pointing to Ivy, "were supposed to faint into your brother's arms," he said as if it was the most obvious thing in the world. "Punishment for messing up my play!" He reached into his pocket and took out two stones. One was ink black and the other was snow white. Both glowed dangerously bright as he brought them closer to a pail of water which had just appeared in front of him.

The others could just watch helplessly as he tossed them in it.

Travix panted and held his sister tighter in his embrace. Claym took their stones out just before they would die because of the lack of oxygen. Just as he had predicted, Travix became silent as he clutched his fainted sister in his arms.

"Excellent! Now, it won't be painful if your acting meets my standards. But if it doesn't," he gestured to the twins, "that'll happen. And you'll end up doing what I want anyway," Claym said smugly.

He then walked over to Evelynda. "Your turn," he singsonged. "Well, I have to admit that Evelynda wasn't really included in my little performance, but Lucas was, since he was my precious sister's mentor. And it's never a good play if there isn't any romance involved, right? Don't worry, I understand everything." He reached into the shell of magic, patted Evelynda's cheek, and was rewarded with a scowl.

"Oh, the tale of a one-sided love!" he continued. "Or should I say *two* parts of one-sided love? Little Evelynda and Lucas were once childhood friends. But soon they became greedy! They wanted their friendship to become something more! However, being the talented wizard as Lucas was, he was chosen in the Taske city council. Parting is such sweet sorrow, and Lucas simply could not bear the idea of leaving his dear Evelynda. To avoid this kind of situation, he decided to make her hate him. Poor Evelynda was devastated when she saw Lucas holding hands with another girl. In the end, Lucas succeeded, but they both knew inside their hearts that they still had feelings for each other. Very strong feelings, I must say. Realizing he was incapable of hiding his emotions anymore, Lucas quit his job and became a merchant at the Grand Taske Market, for he was certain she would be there. Little did they know that admitting their feelings would be that hard. So, their situation ended up like this: endless bickering and fights. Will they finally be true to themselves? Or will they continue this pathetic charade? Definitely a best seller, am I correct?" Claym flashed a smile then sighed. "Now, I don't know how to break you like I did to my little sister, but I do know how to hurt you— physically. I trust that would drive you insane, eh?" he said to Lucas, eyebrows raised high and a smirk in place. Before anyone could react, Claym waved his wand, and Daisy, Cynthiana's cow appeared inside of the room. He whispered something into the cow's ear, and the cow turned around with its backside facing Evelynda. Jessica realized what Claym was planning to do, but her shrill "Watch out! was lost beneath Evelynda's wails of agony.

Daisy had kicked Evelynda squarely in the middle of her chest, causing her to stumble back a few steps and collapse on the floor. The poor old woman was already quite frail from being a captive of the two hags, and a huge kick from a ten-feet tall cow was certainly too much for her aged body.

"Evelynda!" Lucas kneeled beside his old friend, who was now gasping for air. "This is not happening. You are not leaving me," Lucas kept mumbling word of unbelievement, "Can anyone save her?" he asked aloud.

"Lucas......" her voice was barely above a whisper, yet drew everyone's attention on her. "I'm sorry that I kept quarrelling with you. We could have be great friends... perhaps something more"

"You are not dying. You will be alright. Travix. Jessica. Can you do something?" It was more than a question. It was a sincere plead.

"It's okay," Evelynda breathed. "You know the ruled better than anyone. Magic can't be used to bring people back to live. I know that my time is up," she said, her voice growing fainter.

"Don't say that!" Lucas replied fiercely.

"i know it's true. I didn't want to say anything in front of the young ones, but as I saw in my Kuloo, I knew this would happen and am prepared for it. Answer this question," Evelynda could barely speak now, but her eyes remained locked with Lucas's. "Did you ever really....... love me?"

Blinking away tears, Lucas nodded. With a serene smile, Evelynda closed her eyes. Her grip on Lucas's hand slackened and she let out her final breath of air.

Ryan felt a tear drip down his face as her watched Lucas sob silently. Even though he hadn't met Evelynda for a long time, she was always there to help him, and often gave him good advice. He couldn't help feeling sorry that he would never hear Evelynda and Lucas bickering again. It was annoying at first, but after getting used to it, that was actually quite sweet.

"Well done!" Claym's boisterous voice broke the silence. "You all acted according to the script. Now, for out last person," he looked directly at Ryan. "Look at his face, so young, innocent, and carefree."

Ryan wiped the tear away and glared at the man in front of him. "Yeah, and now look at your face, so ugly deformed, and scarred. You look as if you've been clawed by a rabid cat. What did you do to make a cat so mad? I seem very handsome compared to you, right, Jessica?" Ryan answered, a grin spreading across his face as he finished his sentence.

Claym's eyebrow twitched, but he ignored Ryan and kept on saying, "Too bad for such a young lad, who had come to this wretched place unwillingly, and get into such a fishy situation, all because of that foul black box."

"Because you touched it!" Ryan exclaimed. Everyone looked at him questioningly. "Well, he said that the box is foul, and that's because he touched it before sending it to me!"

Jessica couldn't help herself. A small giggle escaped through her lips while she also couldn't hide the smile on her face. Ivy had recovered by then, and both of the twins were trying hard to suppress their snickers too.

A scowl appeared on Claym's face, but for some reason, he didn't do anything to Ryan for all that cheek. He continued, "In this desperate situation, our young warrior had to go to so many perilous places and battle dragons, hags, and all sorts of vile creatures."

"See the creature standing in front of me? Behold the vilest creature ever!" Ryan spread his arms wide, gesturing at Claym exaggeratedly.

At this, even Cynthiana cracked a smile. Jessica, Ivy, and Travix all erupted into laughter. Putting a hand on Ryan's shoulder, Claym glared and growled, "Look, boy....."

"Eww! You touched me! I'm being infected! Jessica, do you have any anti-bacteria soap? I better wash myself before the germs spread all over my body!"

Claym was not amused. "Keep it up, and I'll cut your blasted tongue off before you blink an eye."

"Oooh, so now you're threatening me? Didn't your mommy teach you that it's not nice to threaten others? Bad Claym. Bad!"

A vein throbbed on Claym's forehead. "I warned you," He snarled as flames shot out from his wand, targeting Ryan's chest.

"You do realize that I was made fire proof in your office, right?" Ryan laughed. Then he noticed his bare torso. "Hey! That was my favorite shirt! You burned it on purpose!" His eyes widened. Like a virgin protecting her virtue, he hugged himself and did a very bad imitation of a girl's voice. "Oh, I didn't know, Claym, I never thought you were one of them. I...I should have noticed the moment I saw you. But we can never be together. I mean, I know I am totally hot and all, but I really can't— "

"Enough!" Claym bellowed. "I'm perfectly straight and you know it!" Seeing their doubting looks, he screamed, "I LOVE FEMALES!"

Awkward silence.

The others burst out laughing as his face went so red it could rival a tomato. Even Lucas smiled a bit, smiled a bit, but he still held the forever silenced fortune teller tightly by her hand.

Jessica and the twins knew firsthand how infuriating Ryan could be when he set his mind on annoying people. They actually felt a tiny bit sorry for Claym.

"Stop laughing!" Claym demanded. His protests were soon drowned in their laughter. "I said stop laughing!" he repeated, louder this time. Again, no one paid him any heed. Claym's face grew redder and redder, and a vein bulged on his neck. His fury was obvious, but still, all of them ignored him. Finally, he reached his breaking point. With a huge stomp and a yell of anger, the magic-proof shell encasing them collapsed.

"Geez, and I thought Adrei was the one with mega temper issues," Ryan commented. However, his remark was lost amidst the furious blast Cynthiana fired at Claym. Now that they were able to perform magic, the captives were doing their best to attack. Even Lucas had carefully laid Evelynda in the corner, conjured throwing stars from thin air, and was aiming them at Claym with such accuracy that should be impossible for someone his age. After surveying their situation, Ryan grabbed Mirroride and rushed to join them.

Despite their attempts to harm Claym, he seemed to be protected by a thin layer of light purple glow.

"The orb of energy in the prophecy room will continuously fuel my power. In other words, you cannot harm me, much less break through this barrier, unless the energy orb is destroyed. Which will, quite surely, bring the city of Daske down." Claym said, regaining his smug attitude. "And of course our dear princess wouldn't allow that to happen, yes?"

"Who should I finish first? So far I'm favoring the warrior. Somebody want to volunteer? Anyone?" he called out in a falsely cheerful voice, eyes fixed at Jessica, who had turned paler than a ghost.

"Your opponent is here," Cynthiana snarled. When Claym threw her an uninterested glance, she sneered, "Or are you too scared to get beaten up by your baby sister?"

Claym only shook his head in fake sorrow. "I pity you. What happened to your patience? Very well then. Behold, the death of Cynthiana Lorahas!"

"Wait!" Ivy's voice rang through the room. "How do we know whether they be playing with us or not? Since Cynthiana and *Cee*," she emphasized the name, earning a glare from Claym, "they both be Lorahas, so they both have evil blood running through them!"

"I agree with Ivy. Their histories are both filled with double crossings. We shouldn't trust them." Travix inserted his opinion. Lucas looked hesitant for a moment, but nodded in agreement. "We can't afford to take any more chances," he said regretfully, wand raised high, aiming it at Cynthiana's heart.

Ryan felt someone elbowing his arm. "The letter! Give her the letter!" Jessica whispered fiercely, indicating his backpack.

"Right! Love you, Jess!" Everyone in the room turned their attention to him, to which he immediately blushed. "I mean, I know I can always count on you, Jessica! Yeah, that's all. I didn't mean it *that* way! Stop staring or I'll-"

"Just get on with it, boy," Lucas said calmly.

"A letter...?" Cynthiana murmured softly, her eye clouded with confusion.

"Yep. A letter delivered too late that can hopefully bring back the old you," Ryan said, holding the faded piece of paper to her.

Seeing it, Claym's eyes widened. "Impossible. When I acquired the box from that magician years ago, the first thing I did was to make sure that it was destroyed. This simply cannot be it." In a flash, he snatched the letter away and floated up, standing on a purple glow of energy. A wave of his wand and flames enveloped the paper, turning it into ashes.

But his smirk disappeared when the ashes reassembled and pieced itself back into its original form. The letter floated down slowly and was caught by Cynthiana just before it touched the floor. As she read it, her single eye opened wide, and let out a small gasp.

"That's not all. Here's what was in the box," Ryan said, holding the box out to her. Cynthiana peered inside to see its contents, gently took out the eye, and looked at it closely. To Ryan, it seemed quite bizarre as the two jade green eyes stared at each other.

"What did you do?" Travix whispered to Ryan. "May we see the letter?" Cynthiana, who was staring at her eye as if it was the most valuable object in the world, held out the letter wordlessly. Lucas, Travix, and Ivy all crowded together to read, and Claym, knowing that the letter couldn't be destroyed, didn't stop them, even though they could clearly see him pout as he lowered back to the ground.

"Oh, so you really be nice! Well, nicer than we think you are!" Ivy said in realization, after she finished reading the letter.

"Cruelty turned me into this. I became so obsessed in retrieving my eye, I didn't stop at anything. Now, however, I know exactly who shall I unleash all my ruthlessness on," Cynthiana answered, glaring at Claym. Lucas walked over to her, touched her shoulders gently, and said softly, "I'm sorry that I misunderstood you. After I heard about you and the dark arts, I lost faith in you, and gave up on your original bubbly spirit. I am deeply sorry." Lucas bowed his head then continued, "But it is good to see you so optimistic again. Now, as you said, we have a villain to dispose of."

"Indeed. But first, I need to replace my eye," Cynthiana replied.

"Aww, how sweet!" Claym spat as he once again floated on top of them, venom dripping in his tone. "Oh! Did I interrupt you? I'm so sorry! Go on, just ignore me, keep on pretending that I'm not here!"

"Somebody be jealous of all the attention," Ivy singsonged. Claym glared at her.

"I have a question," Ryan asked. "If you never wanted us to find the letter, then why did you send us on a quest to open it? That doesn't make any sense."

"Of course it doesn't make any sense to you. That little brain of yours would never be able to understand my marvelous scheme. Don't you get it? The prophecy never said that its main purpose was for you to find the key to the black box. It was you who misinterpreted it. I knew the prophecy included that 'the traitor would be unmasked', so I took a wild gamble. To avoid suspicion, I kept both the box and the key away from myself. I passed the box to you, hid the key, and sent you on a journey far away. Once all signs of evidence were gone, not a single person would ever suspect that I, Claym Sonfoe Lorahas, was ever a traitor to Daske!

Besides erasing the signs of betrayal, my plan had other benefits as well. Cynthiana, who had sought out the box for a long time, would never suspect that the 'stupid warrior' had the very item she was seeking. I provided her information about the prophecy, which naturally led to her keeping an eye on you. But she would never expose herself in front of you, for the prophecy mentioned that you would 'destroy the E.Y.E', so that cut down any chance of her to get the box from you. During that time, I was able to completely drain Daske's magic supply and finally get my long-awaited revenge!"

Everyone was silent as what Claym said slowly sank in.

"Well, your *marvelous scheme* didn't work, since we succeeded on opening the box and revealing you as the biggest traitor ever. Hey Clay, whatcha gonna do now? Cool! Your name rhymes with hey! How do you like your perfect little plan messed up?" Ryan taunted.

Claym smiled, but it looked rather forced, making it closer to a grimace instead. "My name is Claym Sonfoe Lorahas, and I do not prefer to be called by a ridiculous nickname. And as for the other question, now that you have all teamed up against me, I think it is only fair that I call my, well, reinforcements. Do not worry, everything is still within my control," he shot back.

All of them tensed as a dark swirl of blackness formed on top of their heads, gradually gaining size. Bright flashes could be seen penetrating through it, while the crackling sounds of lightning became more and more audible.

It had been a long day for the Daske City Council. After the usual paper work and endless meetings between other cities, all ten members were downright exhausted. But they couldn't rest. Not yet. They still had to maintain the power of the purple energy sphere in the prophecy chamber, which was, quite oddly, getting weaker by the day. So they had to buckle up and keep on working.

Harri Moral knew being in the council was a great honor. After all, only ten people could be chosen out of over nine thousand Daske citizens. But sometimes there were just too many things to do, and far too much pressure.

He stretched, rubbed his tired eyes, then sneaked a glance in Zelene Earl's soft green orbs and dark brown hair, which were pulled back into a sensible bun, with only a few tendrils escaping onto her little heart shaped face. He then noticed that his fellow eight coworkers had already headed off to the prophecy room, so now they were the only remainders left.

Now was his chance. His one in a lifetime chance! He had to say it now!

Clearing his throat, he nervously turned to Zelene. "Miss...Miss Earl?"

"Yes, Mr. Moral?" she replied in that sweet voice of hers, turning her attention from the spell she was working on to the anxious man beside her.

"I...I need to tell you something. I really well, really lo— "

A small portal suddenly popped out between them. It was barely half a foot wide, but it caught their attention nonetheless. And just as fast as it appeared, it disappeared almost immediately.

Zelene stared at Harri, startled. "Did you just see a portal?"

He nodded. His expression was identical to hers, but with a hint of exasperation. He couldn't help but think how unlucky he was. Of all the times they were alone, which weren't much, a portal just had to pop out now.

"Darn it," he muttered.

"We should probably stay for a while and check," Zelene suggested, looking concerned. "It's against the law to open a portal in the city without a permission slip. Who knows if someone is trying to break in? What if they stole our files and spell books? There are very valuable works in here, Harri! We cannot let the people of Daske in danger, not when the energy orb is growing weak!" Worry was evident in her eyes, and she had placed both hands on his shoulders when she was talking. Seeing this, Harri's heart almost melted. Not to mention he almost did a happy dance when she addressed him as his first name.

"You worry too much, Z-Z-Zelene. But I agree with you. We should stay here," he answered. Yes! Spending more time with Zelene was like a dream come true!

So they sat down and waited.

"Guys, buy me some time!" Jessica yelled. Claym had summoned a Phantom. Those were among the rarest and darkest creatures in the world. Unlike the Volter Dwarf and the Rockin' Slime Golem, which were more like a joke rather than real danger, Phantoms were in a completely different class of its own. They only had one motivation, and that was to obey every command of its master.

Phantoms also had the ability to posses others. That was the main reason why they were considered dangerous and feared by. It was virtually impossible to regain your consciousness once you were possessed, as least there wasn't any known way to do so.

Travix eyed the Phantom wearily, his wand clutched tightly in his left hand. Sharing a knowing glance with Lucas, they both agreed that their first priority were the ones who couldn't defend themselves. Although Evelynda had left them, they still could not guarantee whether the Phantom could possess her body or not. People knew way too little about the oily black figure hovering in front of them. As for Ivy, if the Phantom did get past him, she could still rely on her reflexes, which in his opinion, were actually pretty good. Of course, he wouldn't give it a chance to try.

"What are you up to?" he yelled back, "You know we cannot portal out!" He couldn't understand why Jessica was making a very small portal and scribbling furiously on a piece of paper from Ryan's pink notebook.

"Travix! It's behind you!" Ryan yelled frantically, motioning him to turn around. The Phantom stood there, its eyes hollow with vast nothingness. It opened its mouth, or at least that was what Travix thought it was, and an unpleasant odor of rotten flesh wafted out, making his eyes water. Sending a flash of lightning to it, he ducked and leapt away.

"Don't let it touch you!" Lucas warned. Out of the corner of his eye, he saw the Lorahas siblings far away from everyone else, and were engaged in a ferocious battle. Claym was still floating on top, which angered Cynthiana.

"Get down here! Stop being a coward!" she demanded. The flames that shot out her wand mirrored those in her eyes.

Claym just laughed. "It is too easy to make you lose your temper. Believe me, I knew that a long time ago, when you were still a five-year-old child. That fit you threw when your plush toy bunny's ear fell off was epic. You seriously need to learn to control your temper. It's a disgrace of our family."

"Disgrace?! What harm have I done to you in –"

"Don't you dare finish that sentence!" he screamed. "What harm have you done? WHAT HARM HAVE YOU DONE?! You wrecked everything! You were probably too young to remember, or you simply chose not to, but the Lorahas family used to be the strongest clan back then. There were three families at that time, Lorahas, Marisole, and Aldos. Everything was balanced, but once you became the one in control, everything just fell apart, and the people just had to blindly follow you. You caused a lot of trouble, and I'm sick of cleaning up the mess you made! You were far too protected, like a fragile set of porcelain. Who spent endless nights doing paperwork and flipping through dull spell books to help our family? Who personally trained an army of warlocks to protect and ensure our position? Who sacrificed all he had for a little brat like you? Me! It's always me! You had everything served on a golden platter right in front of you!" The power of his magic rose rapidly as he finished each sentence until it exploded like an angry volcano.

Ryan could hear Claym's furious rants in the distance, but he wasn't really paying much attention to him. His focus was on the figure that was currently moving ghostly around him. Black threads of darkness swirled around its body, trying to touch him. Every time they got close, he had to slice them in half, but the Phantom was persistent. A blast of energy suddenly burst out from Claym's direction, shaking the ground and sending Ryan tumbling down. He braced himself for the Phantom's attack, only looking up to see it glide soundlessly past him.

Heading straight in the direction of Jessica.

"JESSICA!" he cried in panic. So that had been the Phantom's plan. Once he was distracted, and then was the time it would move to its true target. The one with magic abilities. The one that was too oblivious to the fighting around her because she was concentrating so hard on the portal she was trying to make for some reason.

Jessica sighed. All she needed was a small portal. Was that too much to ask for? She knew that Claym's magic was stopping her, but this was ridiculous. Even a clear Amethyst could make one. She mentally scoffed at how pathetic she was. She was too tired, and the others worried her, diverting her attention. The amount of Dustrix was running low, and she briefly calculated that she had another three or four chances before it completely ran out. Praying for the best, she sprinkled some of the pale golden dust and waved her wand. Bright purple flames danced in front of her, forming the shape of a ring. It was about as wide as her first, but it was more than enough. Overjoyed at the fact that she finally succeeded, she hastily snatched the letter she just wrote, preparing to jam it into the portal.

A sudden feeling of coldness washed upon her, shattering every coherent thought she had, tearing apart her mind. She blinked, and when she reopened her eyes, everything was masked with light gray.

It was almost like an old black-and-white movie, with all the color stripped away. She tried desperately to regain her consciousness, and that was when she remembered the portal. Forcing herself to cram the letter into the portal, she then finally allowed herself to slip into deep and dreamless slumber.

Harri was starting to feel a bit impatient. It had been over an hour since the portal that interrupted his confessions to Zelene appeared. If someone had really tried to break in, he or she should have long given up by now.

"Are you sure you still want to wait, Zelene? I am pretty sure that nothing bad will happen now, except the others might get mad at us if we don't head to the prophecy room right now," he said. "Not that I minded to wait another few minutes," he then added.

"I think you're right," Zelene agreed, standing up and smoothing her wrinkled skirt. "We should get going. I hope they won't be too angry at –"

A soft pop stopped her from finishing her sentence. It was another portal, but this time a piece of paper flew out, floating down the floor.

Bending down and grabbing it, Harri unfolded the paper and started to read it with Zelene.

When they finished it, they glanced at each other and spoke in unison, "This cannot be happening."

"There must be some way to defeat that!" Ryan shouted. He just couldn't accept the fact that Jessica had been possessed by the humongous black figure, more shadow than flesh. He had got to rescue Jessica no matter what. She had saved his skin more times than he was proud of. Now it was Ryan's turn. He owed it to her.

Ryan knew that defeating the Phantom was out of his range, so he decided to let Lucas and Travis handle it, who knew more about the creature. Maybe he could try to distract Claym, or maybe even persuade him to remove it, though he sincerely doubted that would happen. Nah, he'll just go for option one. At least he could stab him in the foot with Mirroride or something.

"Hey Clay!" Ryan yelled across the room. Claym looked up from his argument with Cynthia. "What?" he said irritably.

"Oh, nothing. Just wondering. Is this an authentic Phantom?"

"Yes, of course. You think I would go easy on you?"

"Wouldn't dare to hope for. So you have total control over it?"

"Yes."

"And it's one of the most powerful creatures ever?"

"Yes."

"And it can possess people?"

"Yes! Why are you asking idiotic questions?"

"Hey, I'm a newbie. Give me some info, 'kay? Then this phantom will answer to your every command?"

"Yes!"

"And you're the moron that will remove this hideous creature right?"

"Yes! Wait, no!" Claym, distracted by Ryan and Cynthiana bothering him at the same time, was late in realizing his answer. Cynthiana smirked while Ryan announced, "Everybody listen up! Clay here has just publicly admitted that he is a moron and will remove the Phantom personally!"

"No...I did not say that!" Claym sputtered wildly. He looked furious at himself for not paying close attention to what Ryan was saying at that time.

"Yes you did. I said that you were a moron and would remove the monster, and you said yes before changing it to no. You can't take your answer back once you say it. Ever," Ryan replied, grinning at the sight of Claym's expression of outrage.

Lucas and the twins heard what Ryan just said, momentarily ignored the Phantom, and started to laugh out loud. The joke wasn't even really that funny, but it somehow eased the tension, and for a moment everyone just relaxed, the fear in their eyes disappearing. Even Cynthiana smiled, which only made Claym grow angrier and angrier. It was pretty funny to watch his face turn into different colors. First it was chalky white, then green, then bright red, then finally settling on a purplish eggplant-y color. It was actually quite amazing.

During the time, however, the Phantom was extremely bewildered. All the people that were previously trembling in fear were all laughing uncontrollably, like they didn't even acknowledge its presence. Joy was what the Phantom hated the most, but now the room was filled with it. The Phantom began to shake, trying to get the people afraid again.

Ryan, who was also keeping an eye on Jessica, saw her suddenly tremble wildly. Since she was possessed, it could only be the Phantom's doings. Strangely, the Phantom had been quite silent when they were laughing, and when the laughter subsided, that was when Jessica began to shake. An almost unbelievable idea emerged into Ryan's head.

"All of us keep on laughing! Think of the funniest thought as hard as you can. No matter what, don't stop! If you're not in the mood, watch me!" Ryan began to do a dance he and his classmates made up in school while goofing around. It included moves like shaking his butt exaggeratedly and clapping while stepping side to side. The sight of him was utterly ridiculous, even more so when started to sing "I am such an awesome guy" to the tune of "Mary had a little lamb." Travis and Ivy immediately burst out laughing. Lucas and Cynthiana, however, weren't that amused.

"What are you doing, boy? Now isn't the time for such nonsense!" "Ryan, stop distracting us! We need to focus!"

"No, I *am* thinking seriously! When we were all laughing before, the Phantom had been completely silent, and when we were all panicking, it was all creepy and powerful! I think it preys on fear and hates everything related to happiness! I know this sounds insane, but I have a feeling that this would work!" Now laugh!" Ryan did his dance again, and this time, everybody laughed. Even though Lucas and Cynthiana's smiles were kind of forced, Travis and Ivy were both doubling over in laughter. Ryan's grin was the brightest of all. Forcing himself to temporarily throw his worries away, he concentrated on all his funniest memories, and made himself laugh out loud.

Meanwhile, in the city council, Harri and Zelene were hurrying to the prophecy room. Eight pairs of eyes stared at them as they pushed open the heavy double doors.

"What made you linger so long in the office?" A man spoke up, looking questioningly at them, whom were both panting and had anxious looks on their faces.

"Up to no good, I bet." Another voice replied. Several snickers echoed through the room, but died down immediately, for the purple orb had started to flicker, slowly at first, but gradually becoming more and more rapid. Everyone looked at it worriedly, but Zelene suddenly burst out, "WE know the reason why the orb of energy has been growing weaker lately. Our Princess just sent us a message through a portal. We have always suspected treachery, but never this worse. Read this." She passed the note throughout the room. As each of them read through the passage, the same expression was mirrored on every person's face. Shock.

Jessica couldn't feel a thing. Well, she could, but everything just felt *wrong*. The air shouldn't be that cold, the light shouldn't be that dark, and the uncanny silence surrounding her was just too much for her to bear.

She had just woken up, so her vision was still a tad foggy, and her thoughts were all in a jumble. She looked down to see a swirl of blackness surrounding her ankles, slowly making its way up to her knees. Instantly the lower part of her legs felt numb. Surprised, she tried to move her legs to get rid of the annoying pain, but her legs wouldn't move. She then noticed that her whole body was visibly shaking. She felt like a puppet with strings, controlled by— Something was blocking her thinking. What exactly was controlling her? It's just too tiring to try to remember. She just wanted to go back to sleep. A few minutes wouldn't hurt, right?

She shook her head vehemently. No, she simply would *not* allow herself to quit without trying. Her pride wouldn't allow herself to do so. After all, she was the princess of—

She groaned. Not again. She hated the feeling when she just *knew* she was so close to remembering the answer she was searching for but still couldn't.

Someone stepped in front of her. A face vaguely familiar, perhaps one of her servants that used to take care of her? However, something told her that she was wrong. That person standing in front of her had a grin on his face. It seemed kind of forced, but the smile made her think of special memories. She thought of all the times she had shaken her head in exasperation at that grin. It all felt so long ago. Who is he, exactly?

The person bent down till he was facing directly at her. With a soft voice, he said, "Jessica? Can you hear me? If you can, then please listen to me. Look, the Phantom preys on fear. It hates anything related to happiness. We are all trying hard to create a sense of joy on this room, but I think it will work best if you do too. I know it may be hard, but please try. Think of one memory. Just one. Focus on your happiest thought, okay? I'm pretty sure that we can defeat the Phantom if you can."

Jessica scrunched up her brow in deep concentration. Even though she only understood half of what the boy said, she got that they were in some sort of danger and she needed to think of a happy memory. Her mind still blurred, she forced herself to focus. Strangely enough, all her happiest memories seemed to surround her experiences with a friend. In fact, he was the same person who had just spoken to her! She thought of a time when they had to get through an icy tunnel. She remembered falling on top of him, his lips only mere inches apart of her own. And when she tried to move off him, her heart had threatened to jump out of her chest when his hand on her arm suddenly jerked her back on him again. If possible, his confused look only made him look even more adorable. That, was definitely her happiest memory she could think of just then. She focused on her joy, trying desperately to recall the identity of the person at the same time. Something rather simple and easy to say. Was it Ron? No, it had two syllables.

Ryan! The name rung like a bell inside her head. Jessica was so relieved to remember Ryan's name that she began to laugh out loud. It may sound silly, but she was afraid that if she didn't' remember his name, she would lose this friend forever.

As she laughed, Jessica noticed that the gray veil masking her eyes was gradually shrinking, eventually disappearing altogether. When her vision was finally clear, she saw who she had been thinking of standing right in front of her, grinning.

"Ryan!" Without pausing to think, Jessica stepped forward and slung her arms around him. On an impulse, she kissed him gently on the lips. It was a quick kiss, then she pulled back, suddenly embarrassed at what she just done. Ryan didn't seem to mind, however, he just looked at her, grinned some more, and said, "Do you know how much I did to save you? Where's my reward?"

Jessica couldn't help but smile at Ryan's question. Instead of answering, she kissed him again, longer this time. He returned it with the same affection she gave him, bringing her closer and encircling his arms around her. Leaning forward, she whispered into his ear, "This, is the happiest memory of my life."

Chapter 10

Claym was furious. How, for goodness sake, could the brat Ryan manage to defeat his monster, his perfectly trained Phantom, in a way that had never been heard of? Who would have thought of laughing? Well, maybe it was possible, since the boy never focused on the right things at the right time. He raised his hand, mentally commanding the Phantom to possess another victim without glancing at the creature. After several seconds, Claym didn't feel the dark, cold feeling when the Phantom did to his will. Glancing at it in irritation, he saw it writhing on the floor, trying to shrink to its smallest size.

No wonder it was. Ryan was so proud of himself defeating the Phantom and saving Jessica that he went around the room boasting about his 'incredible and awesome' thinking. Everyone had to admit that Ryan was pretty amazing for thinking up that idea, and was congratulating him merrily. The Phantom couldn't stand the atmosphere and was apparently trying to hide away.

"Look at the Phantom," Travix said as he pushed Ryan away when the boy tried to persuade him to dance with him, "Now would be the perfect time to destroy it."

"I have a better idea," Lucas offered, scratching his chin thoughtfully, "There is very little information about the Phantom, and it would be a great achievement to study it. It truly is an amazing specimen. Does anyone have a container?"

"Be this okay?" Ivy asked, producing an empty nymph melody jar.

"Absolutely. Just cover it first. Phantoms prefer the dark." Travix, eager to escape Ryan's nonstop pleading, rushed over and wrapped his cape around the bottle.

"Would anyone help me? I'm afraid my knees can't take the stress," the old man said as his tried painfully to crouch down and finally surrendering.

"I'll do it," Ryan offered. He squatted down and held the jar close to the Phantom. Sensing the dark, it slowly moved into the jar until it was entirely inside.

"Who's the captive now?" Ryan asked the jar, peering inside. It trembled wildly, startling him for a second.

"Don't do anything rash, boy," Lucas warned. "Let me have it first." He screwed on the lid, and with a wave of his wand, he then handed it back to Ryan, who immediately studied the creature in interest.

"What did you do?" Travix asked, curious.

"Little spell I invented. It's an Anti-breaking charm. Just in case our little specimen tries to break out," Lucas replied.

Ryan stood up and grinned. "Well, if that's taken care of, I believe it's now butt kicking time. Right, Cynth?"

Cynthiana nodded then scowled. "I hate nicknames. They are so—, well, vulgar. I prefer formal manners, meaning the act elegant and graceful at all times."

"Said the bloodthirsty murderer who wiped out a whole city without batting an eye," Travix joked.

"Oh no, Travix, you forgot an essential detail. It's the bloodthirsty murderer who 'elegantly and gracefully' wiped out a whole city without batting an eye," Ryan corrected, making a face.

"You can all joke about proper manners. Just don't come crying when you fail to catch yourself a wife." Cynthiana said, feigning anger. However, the amused glint in her eye gave her away.

During the whole time, Claym was oddly quiet. The former Daske adviser had his eyes downcast, and he seemed to be sweating profusely.

Nobody saw the dangerous gleam in his eyes.

The ten members of the Daske City Council stared mutely at the flickering energy orb. Their goal was clear, but how could they achieve it? It was one thing to maintain energy, but to destroy it? Who ever said breaking was easier than mending?

The orb was unknown to the majority of Daske citizens except for a small number of elders and the higher levels inside the castle, such as themselves. The amount of magic it held was incalculable. Every single spell cast in Daske tapped into its power; it kept the whole city running. Yet when it was summoned and why it was placed in the prophecy chamber was still a mystery.

But now one thing was clear. Painfully clear.

One of the eldest members, Lyzel, stepped forward and cleared his throat. "I remember that the very first rule I knew when I was chosen in the Daske City Council was to never harm the energy orb, and I know it has been the same way for all of you as well. But rule or not, we have to destroy it before the traitor gains any more power." He paused. "We have to perform that spell."

The spell he was referring to was a level dark diamond complex. Complex spells, referring to their names, were more complex than simple ones, and they required more than one person to perform. Which, in this situation, required ten.

"I shall begin the spell," Lyzel volunteered. "I'm sure that the rest of you all know the process, no?" The nine people nodded mutely in return. "Good. So after I start, come in during your parts at the right moment. Is everything clear?"

Lyzel was considered as the leader of the council, partially because of his age and the ability to stay calm and take charge in an emergency. No one ever questioned his right of power and he had proved he was capable, so naturally it was his job to lead the spell that consisted of so much responsibility.

The lights of the prophecy room were turned off, the only source of light coming from the glowing purple energy orb.

Tension was thick in the air. The ten members formed a circle around the orb, which was flickering intensely. Eyes never leaving the ball of energy, Lyzel took a step forward and began to recite:

> *Here we stand, with all our might*
> *Hoping to try and set things right*
> *For now, the time has arrived.*
> *The time we've been dreading of,*
> *The time we've been fearing of,*
> *The time, we wished would never come…*

Dark purple light, the exact same shade as the orb, shone from the tips of each member's wand, growing brighter as everyone joined in the spell.

> *…We know not of what will happen.*
> *What shall be the price of this action?*
> *Pandemonium, fiascos, and chaos may threaten,*
> *Yet in this troubled moment,*
> *Here we stand,*
> *Relieving the kingdom from its depression.*

There was a solemn moment when the spell was finished. Each member of the council was silent, barely even breathing, in hopes that the spell would work.

That complex spell was invented for times when Daske was in danger. It was a spell that had powerful destruction powers, and was used only in the utmost emergencies because it drained huge amounts of magic from the orb. It actually served their purpose. The spell was only able to demolish a single object, but theoretically it would destroy anything, no matter how powerful it is, which, in this case, was the purple energy orb of Daske.

Suddenly, a blazing glare flashed through the great prophecy room, shockingly bright. Everyone took a step back, each raising a hand to block it. The orb was the source, and after a full minute, the light died down completely, revealing only an empty pedestal where the orb used to hover upon. The members let out a collective sigh of relief. No harm was done. Every person was safe, and the power of the orb was gone.

Then someone screamed. Deep purple flames were erupting out of thin air, burning up the curtains of the room, spreading rapidly to the other parts of the castle. Whoever invented the spell knew about the price to pay. There was a fiasco after all.

In spite of its unusual color, the flames also caused more damage than regular fires did. No one had ever seen anything like it before. This wasn't just any normal magical fire. With every second it burned, it blazed even brighter.

And the ten members of the Daske City Council could only stand dumfounded and watch in complete horror as the flames spread throughout the castle.

Something is wrong, Ryan noted. Maybe it was the sudden change of atmosphere in the air, the tension being so thick he could practically cut off a piece from it. But the real thing that was off-balance was that Claym was smiling.

It wasn't a small smile of defeat, not the ones that were bitter and usually accompanied with a sigh, but a full-fledged, cocky, I-know-something-you-don't-know smile.

"My, my. What a sacrifice you've made, princess. Very bold and efficient, I give you that, but what about the consequences? It is so not like you to endanger your people," Claym said, his trademark sneer once again found its way to his lips.

Jessica seemed to grow paler every moment. "Con-consequences? What consequences? The spell should have—I can't believe—What have I done?" She buried her face in her hands, eyes wide open.

The glass jar in Lucas's hands shook.

With a grin that could almost rival the Cheshire cat's, Claym continued mercilessly, "Exactly 'what have you done', princess! It was very clever of you to think of cutting off my power supply. I must admit that I never thought you'd take that gamble. But sadly I already installed my last attack during the time you were joking around about manners. My deepest gratitude to you, Ryan," he smirked then continued, "So it is quite certain that the whole castle and part of the city are engulfed by flames by now. Really, I expected better of you." He paused, and then slyly added, "You people expected better of you."

The last sentence was like a hard punch delivered to Jessica's stomach. With each verbal blow, she grew more and more distraught, but that only seemed to make Claym grin wider.

"Oh well, I suppose it's not completely your fault. After all, the Council shouldn't place all the responsibility on a fourteen-year-old girl. Don't' be too hard on yourself. If you ask me, I'd say it's totally out of your capability. They should've known better. Youth and enthusiasm will never best age and treachery." Claym snorted and continued, "They should choose *me* as their next leader if they have any sense. I'm intelligent, cunning, ambitious, responsible, courageous..."

Ryan spaced out to what Claym said after the fifth adjective to describe how magnificent and brilliant he was. Instead, he turned his attention to Jessica. The princess of Daske looked simply miserable. From her drooped shoulders to her lowered head, he couldn't see any sigh of the previous witty yet sweet girl. A flicker in the corner of her eye caught his attention. It was like watching a train wreck; he wanted so bad to turn his eyes away but simply couldn't, and just stood there frozen in horror. He watched the thin layer of mist veiling her watery blue eyes form a single tear, slowing rolling down her delicate porcelain cheeks, then falling down to the floor with a crystal-like twinkle.

He suddenly felt a surge of anger.

"Stop," he murmured his voice barely above a whisper. However, he successfully caught everyone's attention. Well, everyone except the oblivious Claym, who miraculously hadn't run out of praises for himself yet.

"...and to top all that, I'm extremely handsome. Well, that and no one can possibly deny I'm very talented. Oh, and people simply cannot ignore the fact that I'm—" Claym's eyes widened at the wickedly sharp blade right in front of his throat. If not for the purple glow protecting him, he would be long dead.

Claym took a deep breath to recompose himself. He could feel his energy slipping; he only managed to salvage a tiny portion of magic before the orb was destroyed. Nevertheless, he knew he still had ample time before he was completely drained. Although some sly attack was the best offense, it had too much at stake, and he was never the one to act on impulse. Let them attack all they want; he still had one more trick up his sleeves.

Cynthiana seized the opportunity to summon a tornado towards him, which Lucas's blast of lightning quickly followed. However, their combined attack didn't seem to weaker Claym's protection, if not, it seemed to grow even stronger. That was his trick. He willed the energy around him to absorb any magic sent towards him, and their attacks were certainly magical. Claym smirked. His instincts never failed him, and he knew this was a battle he should easily win.

Ryan, on the other hand, had different ideas. The anger swelling in his chest quickly morphed into something more as Claym added layer after layer of protection around himself. His eyes narrowed into slits when he registered a foreign feeling.

Though he often acted like an over-excited idiot, Ryan was actually a pretty laid back guy. He seldom lost his temper, and he believes in a philosophy that everything eventually would turn out right. Yet, the little spark of anger ignited by Claym was now turning into a forest fire.

Mirroride glowed, and he suddenly knew what to do. A wave of fury washed through him. Without thinking, Ryan plunged the sword into Claym's heart.

The moment the sword came in contact with Claym, it gave off such a brilliant glare that they were forced to shield their eyes. As soon as it dimmed, Claym slumped onto the floor, already gone. There was a flash of purple light, and the corpse vanished into nothingness.

Chapter 11

People were panicking. The magical fire had wrecked much of the castle and spread across the city within a few minutes. None of the people had the slightest notion on how the fire started, and were mostly frozen in place, stricken, or scrambling around in terror. The few who knew bits of magic tried desperately to put it out, yet their feeble attempts didn't slow down the fire at all. In fact, their magic seemed to fuel it and cause it to grow even stronger.

The members of the city council knew that it was their responsibility to set things right. However, they were torn apart between two decisions. Should they contact Princess Jessica? So far none of them succeeded on getting in touch with her. It was like she and her companions simply vanished, lost in a remote space that no portal could reach. Or should they focus on putting out the fire first? The city would most surely be ruined if they didn't stop it immediately.

"We have no way of extinguishing the fire. It becomes stronger when magic is used, and water has no effect on it at all. Our priority is to contact our princess, but her whereabouts are unknown to us. In other words, we are unable to accomplish anything at this moment. We have failed to protect out city. We failed our promise to the people," Lyzel said, fatigue evident on his face strewn with ash smudges. He shook his head as the wall with Ryan's prophecy crashed to the floor. If Lyzel was admitting defeat, then there really was no hope at all. The rest of the members hung their heads in silence, praying for a miracle of the slightest chance to happen.

Five minutes later, their prayers were answered. As sudden as it arrived, the fire abruptly died into nothingness. Except for the damage done to the castle, there was no sign that a fire had been in there at all.

There was a popping sound, and a portal appeared in the middle of the prophecy room. All ten members were surprised to see Princess Jessica step out. Behind her emerged two boys and girl around their age, an old man, whom Lyzel vaguely recalled as a powerful magician who eventually retired to the Grand Taske Market, and former enemy of Daske, Cynthiana Lorahas. Despite the fact they knew Cynthiana wasn't really their nemesis, the council couldn't help but keep their guard up when she was around. With such odd companions, the princess must have quite a story to tell.

Jessica looked around the castle. Seeing the grand castle in wreckage with shards of glass and broken rubble, she gave an audible gasp. Tears began to water in her eyes, making her seem like a vulnerable little girl instead of the princess who radiated with confidence as she led her city towards prosperity.

Ryan reached out and pulled her close to him, feeling the need to comfort her. At first she struggled against his embrace, trying to stay strong, but he held on tight. Finally she broke down completely, sobbing against his shoulders.

For a long while everyone was silent as they watched the pair entwined with each other, the girl crying, the guy stroking her hair in an awkward yet sweet manner. Eventually Jessica pulled away from Ryan, turning to face the council. Travix, Ivy, Lucas, and Cynthiana came to stand around her, while Ryan stood closely by her side.

Jessica took a deep breath before starting to talk, "For the past ten days, many changes had come upon us. In the process, our city and the magic energy supply protecting it had been destroyed, yet we've found out the person behind who caused so much disaster. Some of you know the recent events of our story, but most of our experience is still a puzzle to you. I would like to share it with everyone, and then we can decide what to do once you have the whole viewpoint."

"This is Ryan. Ryan...What is your full name, anyway?" Jessica asked, turning towards him.

"My name's Ryan Wexler."

"This is Ryan Wexler, and he was brought here by Cee to fulfill a prophecy, the one which mentioned a traitor. It began ten days ago, when he accidentally ran into me outside the castle borders at midnight." Jessica ignored the stares of concern and surprise, and continued on her story. She talked about how Ryan became fireproof ("I hate microwaves," Ryan had muttered), and how they started their quest immediately the next day. Their encounter with the violet-eyed twins, Travix and Ivy, ("Admittedly we were sent by Cynthiana," Travix said. "That woman be horrible to us." Ivy complained. "But now she be nice," she quickly added to Cynthiana who was conveniently standing right next to her) the wonder they felt when they saw all the items at the Grand Taske Market ("Remind me to get a few more Color Splashes," Ryan interrupted)...not a single detail escaped Jessica's photographic memory, and was weaved into her breathtaking story.

Everyone was hanging at her words when she described meeting with the dragons. Ryan stepped in and recalled his moments in the Dragon Rider

Obstacle Course. A few gasps were emitted when the council heard that their next destination was Volcano Acrakk, and then sighed with pity when Evelynda was buried by the sandstorm after they arrived at the Land of Red.

Then came the separation of the two groups. Ryan recounted his terror when he was dangling under the boulder at the Lake of Darkness ("Keeping one or two magical items on hand is certainly a must,"), and Travix described the battle at the EYE headquarters so vividly that the listeners could clearly see the glittering magic-proof walls and chuckle at Nausicaa's temper tantrum as if they were really there. ("You're right, Ryan. *I'm* now a fan of Color Splashes too," Travix agreed)

Jessica went on with the story, talking about the obstacles in the Tunnel of Ice (Ryan and she both turned suspiciously red), how they solved riddles in the Chamber of Fire. At this point, Ryan interrupted, and to everyone's surprise, told them that the dainty silver key was actually a charm that Cee gave him before the journey. ("He thought we wouldn't be able to find the key if it wasn't originally from inside the chamber," Ryan clarified. "But we got the better of him.")

The story continued. The outrageous beauty contest with the hags ("I won't ever let you do my makeup again," Jessica added, shooting a playful glare at Ryan), Aladar the crazy maedella ("I actually kind of liked that guy. What? He's funny." Ryan said), saving Evelynda ("The hags were *crazy* after their makeover," Jessica said, laughing. "They were hot," Ryan added. Jessica then smacked him on the head. Hard), and finally reuniting with the others. After reuniting, Jessica mentioned how Cynthiana was the villain at first, but after Cynthiana called Claym for backup, he changed his appearance and betrayed them all. Everyone was hurt some way during the encounter, especially Lucas. When Jessica came to that part, the old man bushed away a single tear, but remained calm.

"As for the rest of the story, I believe you all know, for I sent a message through a portal just before I got possessed by the Phantom," Jessica said. "And all the thanks go to Ryan for retrieving me from the monster's grasp. As for Claym, we're now done with him, but I will still need your assistance on what our next step should be."

Lyzel stepped forward and bowed deeply. "Princess Jessica, you and your friends have been through more dangers then we could ever imagine. It is time for you to take a break and leave the rest to us. You have my word that everything will be restored and back to normal in no time," he said. Turning around to face the council members, Lyzel commanded, "Casir and Thana, the pair of you shall go to Claym's mansion. Search it thoroughly and take notice of anything unusual. If there is need to study something further, bring it back to the laboratory. The remaining eight of us will focus on reconstructing our city. It will be a tremendous work, even with magic, since we would have to summon another magical orb. Zelene and Harri will go around the city for volunteers. It doesn't matter whether they know magic or not; any pair of hands would be a big help to us at this point. As you go, seek out the wounded and bring them to the hospital. You are granted to summon portals if necessary. Report back to us as soon as possible."

Harri stole a glance at Zelene, her green eyes determined as she gave a single nod. He was quite lucky to get paired with her. Considering how well they worked together back in the office, maybe he *could* use the chance to take their relationship up another level.

Lyzel clapped his hands together, "Okay, everyone off to their destinations. If my calculations are correct, it will take us at least six months to rebuild. It's a hard job, but we will need to take full responsibility and restore our city back to normal."

One by one, the members exited, leaving Ryan and the others standing in the middle of the damaged prophecy room.

"Hey. Isn't this my prophecy?" Ryan spotted a piece of the marble wall on the floor, carved with the words that made such a big difference in his life during the past few days.

"A warrior of Earth shall come to Daske," he read aloud, "That's me, then 'Destroy the EYE, traitors unmask'. Well, the EYE is destroyed now, ever since Mr. Claym I-am-a-traitor Lorahas was unmasked." Cynthiana nodded regretfully as Ryan looked at her.

"Exile You for Eternity was a bad idea, I admit, and not just because of the name. However, one thing that I miss is the power I used to control. I'll confess that I am power-hungry and need the feeling of superiority over people. I wish that I can still be the leader of something even though EYE has already crumbled," Cynthiana said with the slightest trace of embarrassment.

Jessica, as the Princess of Daske, stepped over to her and said, "I can arrange that. Even though you've done quite a lot of harm in the past, you still contributed much in defeating Claym. I know you can be trusted now, but people would still tremble when they hear your name. That is why I am offering you a job as a teacher in the Daske School of Weaponry. Weapons are your element, and you will have students to rule over. We will talk about better conditions once you've proved to everyone that you can be trusted."

Cynthiana scowled, but managed to smile reluctantly. "It's the best I can hope for at this point," she said,

Ryan was still busy with the prophecy. "'With luck, the things he seek release, to their rightful owner, the truths unleash.' Many of the things I sought out were released, but I think that this is talking about Cynthiana's eye, which is back to its rightful owner now. Plus, during the process, we learned the truth about Cynthiana's background and Claym's betrayal. So that," he said, looking very satisfied with himself, "is what I call a prophecy well fulfilled."

"Wait. We still have one more thing to seek and return to their rightful owner," Travix said, looking directly at Cynthiana. Ivy caught on and glared at her until Cynthiana couldn't ignore them any longer.

"What?"

"Our life stones. When are you returning them?" Travix asked.

"Weren't they with Claym when he tried to drown you?" Ryan asked, confused, "I saw him slip them into his pocket afterwards."

"Listen to the boy. I no longer have any connections with the stones," Cynthiana said, putting up her hands in surrender.

However, Travix and Ivy weren't fooled by her act. "When Claym vanished, I saw you wave your wand and summon something towards you. From the shape and colors I could make out even with the blinding lights, those looked exactly like our life stones," Travix said indignantly.

Cynthiana couldn't pretend anymore. Like magic, she produced the stones from nowhere and held them out to the twins, one on each palm. Ivy rushed forward and snatched it from her hand immediately, while Travix was slower, carefully turning it around in his hands as he returned to his spot.

"I'm sorry for tricking you, but I just wanted to see your reactions. I'll have to admit that the pair of you have grown a lot during this experience. If this happened before the quest, Ivy would've burst out into tears while Travix just stood there glaring at me. None of you would have dared to talk back." Cynthiana smiled.

"Now we can save our tribe!" Ivy cried happily, holding her stone close to her heart.

"Right. With a bit of assistance, we can definitely undo the curse," Travix agreed.

Lucas, who had been quite silent during the whole time, spoke up, "Now that everyone is happy, I don't think I am needed here anymore. I must return to my little cottage and tend to my affairs."

"You're leaving?" Ryan exclaimed. "But we need you to get me get back home! Not that I really want to go back..." he muttered.

"A portal into another world is hard to make, and only allows one to return to his or her world. You must do it yourself," Lucas said. "Basically the process is the same, but the one returning must have a strong will and focus on the destination. The connection between the two worlds will be weak, so the harder you concentrate, the easier a portal will appear. Be warned. This isn't as easy as you might think. Quite a number of people have been trapped between worlds, unable to get to either side."

Ryan took a step forward with a look of concentration on his face. "I can do this."

Travix sprinkled the golden Dustrix on the floor and waved his wand. Ryan closed his eyes and thought about his room, his huge bed, even the annoying Mrs. Abdullah watching soap operas in the living room. He could feel a kind of energy tugging at him, surrounding him, forcing him to open his eyes. What he saw made him gasp out loud.

Instead of the purple portals Ryan was so accustomed to seeing, a luminous white one was in front of him, giving off such a bright glare that it surprised him.

"Wow," Jessica breathed out the single word. The twins and Cynthiana were staring at it in awe. Even Lucas was impressed. "This portal appeared much faster than normal, and the boy's unusual flow of energy must have been the cause."

Ryan looked at everyone in turn and said, "You guys are the friends and family I never had in my old life. I'll really miss you." He looked at them again, trying to memorize each person's features so he could remember them forever. Lucas's kind eyes and Evelynda's smile, Cynthiana's stunning beauty and shockingly green eyes, the silky pale blond hair and lavender eyes of the twins, and Jessica. With her ice blue orbs and long raven locks, Ryan knew that no other girl would cease to attract him as long as he had the memory of her. She smiled, so tenderly that Ryan felt like his heart was melting. He walked over and gave one last final kiss. "I'll always remember you," she whispered softy into his ear.

Forcing himself to pull away, Ryan walked towards the shiny portal. He turned back to his friends, grinned, and then walked through the entrance that would take him back to reality.

Chapter 12

Ryan opened his eyes. He was lying spread-eagle on his bed, blankets in a tangle around his feet. Rubbing his eyes blearily, he looked around his room. Everything was in place, and he could hear Mrs. Abdullah watching her soap opera loudly downstairs. Life was just as normal and boring like he was used to.

"What an amazing dream," he said aloud, "Wish my whole summer could be like that." As he spoke, he glanced at the backpack under his desk. Its appearance was similar to the one he used in his dream. Too similar, for that matter. Ryan got up and walked over to pick it up. He could see the scorched parts when he entered the Chamber of Fire. Not quite believing his eyes, he opened the bag and dumped the contents onto the floor. The pink notebook and pen Jessica used to crack the code fell out. On the notebook was Jessica's delicate handwriting, persuading Ryan that the journey was for real. To convince himself further, Ryan emptied the pack, dumping its contents on the bed. Two Color Splashes bounced out. Smiling, Ryan put those into his drawer. The slimy colored balls would come in handy while pulling pranks on Roger and the gang.

There was one more object inside the backpack. Ryan thrust in his hand, but when he felt what it was, he gently lifted it out. It was the final unused jar of nymph melodies. The jar with a silver glow like moonlight. Ryan set it carefully on his bureau, where it gave off a soft light.

If everything he used back in Daske had come to Earth with him, then where was Mirroride, his trusty sword? Ryan scanned the room again, finally finding the sword leaning against the wall. He left it there, reminding himself to ask someone to nail a small shelf on the wall where he could display Mirroride.

Turning his attention back to the jar of melodies, Ryan's curiosity got the better of him. He held the silver jar in his hands and slowly twisted the lid open. A single note, a high C played by a flute, filled his bedroom. The jar glowed brilliant white just like the portal which he used to return.

Gradually, the light became so bright that Ryan had to close his eyes against the blazing light. Even if he did, he could still feel the radiance of the light trying to penetrate through his eyelids. When the light finally dimmed, Ryan opened his eyes only to stand with his mouth wide in shock.

Jessica, Travix, and Ivy were standing in the middle of his bedroom, looking around with interest. When Jessica saw Ryan, she gave a little squeal of excitement.

"Ryan! The craziest thing happened. After you, Lucas, and Cynthiana had already gone, we were just about to check on the people when suddenly a blazing white light surrounded us and brought us here! Is this your world? Did you call us?"

Ryan was a bit slow to recover. He stammered. "It's... It's you. I just opened our remaining jar of nymph melodies. A portal appeared... and so did you." Then he grinned, a sight Jessica had grown so accustomed. She couldn't help but smile back when he said, "Well, so much for the little farewell speech I said two minutes ago. I mean, you're all here."

"How are we going to get back?" Travix asked. Jessica nodded in agreement, "My citizens would worry if their Princess disappeared without any warning."

Only Ivy was undisturbed by the fact that they may not be able to return back to Daske. She was peering at his television set with a look of fascination on her face. "What be this?" She asked, "Be this a mirror? I see my reflection!"

"Um...no. It's a television. You watch programs on it," Ryan answered.

"Cool! Can we explore here?" Ivy said excitedly. Jessica and Travix were also showing curiosity in all of his belongings. Jessica was checking out his sound systems and playing with his headphone. Travix was in his en suite; he could hear the faucet running. At their reaction, Ryan got a spark of inspiration.

"I have a better idea. Why don't you just stay here until we find out a way to send you back? There is more than enough space for you to live in, and I can lead you into my life just like you did to me. Daske is in the midst of rebuilding, so you'll need to find new living quarters anyway. My parents won't mind at all. Trust me."

Ivy looked positively delighted, while Travix poked his head out from the bathroom and nodded in agreement. Only Jessica was concerned. "My people and the council will be worried."

"That old guy in the council told you to take a break," Ryan reminded her gently, "In a way, you are. Don't you want to spend more time with me?" He teased her, "I thought you liked me."

Jessica blushed, but was unable to conceal the smile on her face, "Okay, you win," she said, kissing Ryan gently on his cheek. "Anyway, I can go back to Daske wherever I want as long as I have you, right? With your ability in creating wondrous portals, I have complete faith in you."

It was Ryan's turn to blush. Trying to hide his embarrassment, he turned to Travix and said, "Hey, dude. Wanna meet my mates? I'll introduce you to the gang."

"What is this 'dude' you're referring to? I don't understand." Travix looked thoroughly confused.

Ryan grinned, "Man, you want to join us, you gotta learn our ways of living, including our use of slang. Most of all, you have to ditch those breeches and that shirt. People would think that you were crazy if you wore that out onto the street. Try this," he said, tossing a black T-shirt and a pair of jeans to Travix. "You, too," he said to the girls, "I think that my cousin Alyssa left some of her clothes here since her last visit. You can wear them for now, but I'll arrange a shopping trip for you three as soon as I can. Once you've all finished changing, I'll take you out to meet my friends and go out for ice cream. If you need anything, don't hesitate to ask. Meanwhile, I've got to make a very important phone call. Be back to you in five minutes." He then grabbed his iPhone from his desk.

Closing his bedroom door, Ryan slowly made his way to the kitchen for refreshments. Passing the living room, he said to Mrs. Abdullah, "Going out with my friends later," who nodded and went back to her show. As he walked, he couldn't believe how different his summer was going to turn out than he originally imagined. He had friends that would accompany him through life and death, a girl who might have a close relationship with him given time, and an experience in another world he would never forget. The best part, he had the whole summer in front of him to enjoy with his friends, both old and new. He dialed and called his best friend, Roger.

"Hey, Roger, want to hang out later? Call up the gang and we'll meet at the ice cream shop across the corner. I have a couple of friends for you guys to meet. Oh, by the way, I met this girl......"

Portal To Daske—— Secrets of the EYE

作　　者／梁宇絢（Jennifer Liang）、張瓅心（Kelly Chang）

圖文排版／梁宇絢（Jennifer Liang）、張瓅心（Kelly Chang）

封面設計／林揚瀚、梁馨云

出版發行／梁宇絢（Jennifer Liang）
701 台南市東區崇德十六街 13 號
電話：+886-910-274-717
cliang@mail.chna.edu.tw

印製機構／秀威資訊科技股份有限公司
114 台北市內湖區瑞光路 76 巷 65 號 1 樓
電話：+886-2-2796-3638　傳真：+886-2-2796-1377
http://www.showwe.com.tw

ISBN: 978-957-43-0871-2

出版日期：2013 年 09 月初刷
定價：150 元